Wishing that I Was Yours 2

Sherri Marie

Shannon

"One, two, three, shock! One more time! One, two, three, shock! We got a steady heart beat! Ms. Baker, can you hear me? If so, blink your eyes."

My eyes were so heavy, and my body was so weak I could barely blink. I couldn't remember what happened to me after the doctor called my name. I passed right back out I was so drained.

"God, I'm so sorry. Please forgive me. I promise I will make this right, don't take my girl and baby from me please," Gee cried out as he held my hand at my bedside. I gained the strength to move my hand to let Gee know I was okay and I could hear him. "Shannon baby, you okay? Thank God! He heard my prayers!"

"Yes, what happened," I said in a raspy voice. My mouth was so dry I could barely talk.

"That bitch Blaze shot you twice. But don't worry about it, I'm going to make sure she pays for what she did."

I couldn't even gain the energy to reply. I just needed to rest for a while. The next morning when I opened my eyes, Gee was sitting next to me with his head down.

"Good morning, Gee," I said in a low-toned voice.

"Good morning. I love you. I'm sorry, Shannon. I'm so sorry."

"You don't have to apologize, it's not your fault. It's mine. Let's just put everything behind us and start over."

"We can do that." Gee leaned over and kissed me on my forehead.

I started having flashbacks. All I could picture was Blaze aiming her gun at me. I was terrified. They say things happen for a reason and that's true. I was just about to lose the man I loved for good, all because I was lusting for someone I didn't love. But I got my man back. Even though I know it's going to take a lot of trust and rebuilding to get things where it used to be, I'm more than happy to make it work.

After spending almost two weeks in the hospital, the doctor finally released me to go home, after he made sure the baby was fine. When I arrived home, I was so excited. Gee even planned me a welcome home party. All my family and friends were there, including Chaos and Kandi.

"How you feeling, sis? "Chaos asked happily as he came over and gave me a big hug.

"I'm just blessed to be here with my family and friends." I gave a big smile.

"We got a surprise for you," Kandi said, with a big ass grin on her face.

"You know I don't like surprises, Kandi."

"Well, you're going to like this one." Kandi looked at me with a sneaky look on her face.

"Okay, what is it? Damn, y'all got me."

Everyone starts laughing.

"Surprise! You can come out now," Kandi yelled.

Who are they trying to surprise me with? I thought. I looked up and I couldn't believe it! It was my nigga, TK. That's Kandi's boyfriend who just did a bid in jail for bodying a nigga. We were close like brother and sister.

"Oh my goodness! TK, is that you? Oh, my God!"

I couldn't lie, I was super excited to know my brother had stepped down. I ran up to him and gave him the biggest, longest hug ever.

"Don't act like you happy to see me." TK laughed and hugged me back.

"I'm here to stay this time, sis."

"You better be," I replied with a sarcastic, but serious look on my face.

"Come on, y'all, let's celebrate! My wifey's home finally! And I also want to make an announcement. We're getting married in two weeks, and everybody better have they ass there," Gee stated as he pointed his finger at the crowd.

"We will be there, nigga," Chaos shouted, holding his cup in the air.

We all partied! We had spades games going, dominoes, karaoke, drinks, food, and more. I was so exhausted Gee had to carry me to the room. I woke up to him eating my pussy like breakfast. It felt so wonderful, I moved my slippery wet pussy up and down his face.

He started tongue fucking me and put his index finger in me at the same time. It felt so amazing I buried his face in my pussy to make sure all my juices got on his face. Then, he bent me over and fucked me from the back. He had me so wet and horny. Every time he hit it, I could feel my juices splashing on him.

After making love to Gee, I felt so good. We fell asleep and held each other through the night.

The sun beaming in my eyes through my window woke me up the next morning. I rolled over to give Gee a hug, but he was nowhere to be found. I got myself together and started walking downstairs. I could hear Chaos and TK's voices.

"Man, how we going to take this bitch Blaze out?" Chaos asked.

I stopped where I was and listened to the conversation.

"Y'all know we got to play everything cool because I'm not going back to jail," TK replied as he took a hit from his Kush joint and passed it to Gee.

"Ain't nobody going back to jail. Look, I got a plan." Gee started whispering, telling Chaos and TK what the plan was. I could barely hear what was being said, but I did hear some of the plan.

"Good morning, everyone," I said, making my way down the stairs.

"What up," they said in unison.

"Why you're not resting, Shannon? You know what the doctor said. You and my baby need plenty of rest."

"Gee, I laid in the hospital bed for two weeks. I just need to move around a little."

"That understandable, but don't do too much moving. I need a healthy baby"

"Okay, Gee."

Gee was acting very overprotective of me and his baby and I had to admit I was loving it. I wanted revenge on Blaze just as badly as everyone else did, so them plotting against her didn't bother me. Blaze had it coming. She shot me twice, once in the stomach and once in the arm. But that bitch only got a graze in the arm. I'd been plotting on Blaze since I opened my eyes in the hospital. She almost took me and my unborn baby's lives. She's going to pay for what she did and that's a promise. Even though she got locked up and was out on bond, that's not enough for me.

"Shannon, I'm about to go meet up with a client. I will be back shortly to take care of you. In the meantime, if you need anything, Chaos will be here."

"Gee, I don't need a baby sitter"

"Baby, look, I don't know what this bitch Blaze is capable of. I need to protect you at all times," Gee said as he grabbed my face and looked me in my eyes.

"Okay, I understand."

Gee and TK left. I didn't know what Gee was up to, but I knew for a fact he wasn't going to meet up with a client. I went up to my room to get some rest. About two hours later, I got a text from an unknown number saying, *Bitch, this shit ain't over*. I knew it was Blaze, but I didn't reply. She wasn't even worth it. Her death sentence was coming soon anyway. I called Chaos up to my room and told him what Blaze had just texted to me. He told me not to stress about it because it's already taken care of.

"Chaos?"

"What's up, sis?"

"I want this bitch dead. I know what I did was wrong, but I can't knock the fact this bitch shot me and Gee."

"Sis, I feel you, but you pregnant. You got to let us handle this. We got you, believe me."

"If y'all don't handle it, I will, and that's a promise that won't be broken."

"Trust me, we got you, sis. Get some rest."

Chaos walked out the room and went back downstairs.

Gee

"This nigga Cage we about to meet up with, I been knowing him for years. He be on some murder-murder kill-kill type shit," I said to TK as we waited for Cage to pull up to the bar.

I hadn't hit my nigga Cage up in a minute, but desperate times called for desperate measures. I know two wrongs don't make a right, but Blaze had it coming and she was going to feel my wrath. Shannon was my world. Even though she hurt me to the fullest, I still love her. The thought of almost losing her and my unborn child for the rest of my life didn't sit right me at all.

"Ahy. Is that's your boy Cage right there," TK said, snapping me out of thoughts.

"Yeah that's him," I put my hand out the window and hand signaled Cage to go into the bar. Me and TK followed him. When we got in the bar, Cage was sitting in the back. Cage dressed like a business man anytime he conducted business. He had on an all-gray Kiton K-50 suit with some expensive dress shoes on.

"What up, my G," I said as I shook Cage's hand and took a seat.

"What up. Who is this with you? You know I don't handle business like this," Cage responded and mugged TK.

"This my brother TK. He cool people," I said.

"I would rather handle my business with just me and you, Gee."

"No problem. TK, walk away for a minute, brah." I could tell TK wasn't feeling Cage by his facial expression.

"I got a bad feeling about him, brah," TK said under his breath as he walked away.

"Now tell me everything I need to know."

"Well, I got shot and the same bitch that shot me shot my girl in the stomach and she pregnant."

"So, what's my mission? You want this bitch dead or paralyzed?" Cage asked, puffing his Cuban cigar.

"Off that bitch," I replied.

"What you know about this chick so far?"

"She a stripper down at Dream Girls. She goes by the name Blaze, but her real name Blake. She drives a gray Benz truck. She got another car, but I don't know what kind, "I said in a low tone.

"Alright, I'll hit you up soon, Gee."

"Alright," me and Cage shook hands and we went our separate ways.

"TK, Cage cool people," I said as I joined TK at the bar.

"Man, I don't like him. I get a bad vibe from him, Gee. I'm just keeping it real with you, my nigga."

"I understand that, but I'm telling you he good. Just trust my word, I wouldn't trust just anybody."

"True. Alright," Me and TK had a couple of drinks and left, headed back to my spot. When I pulled up to my spot, Chaos was sitting outside smoking a joint.

"Everything good, Chaos?" I asked as I walked up to my front door.

"Yeah, everything Gucci. But Shannon did tell me that that bitch Blaze been threatening her."

"Don't worry about it, it's taken care of," I said as I walked into my house.

I went upstairs and check on Shannon. She was knocked out. I love Shannon, she's my world. Even though she crushed my heart, I learned to forgive her. I took Shannon through some shit in my past with all types of hoes, so it's only right I forgave her for what she did. I can't lie, I never thought I would forgive Shannon, but we all make mistakes. Shannon's a good woman, and I would be a fool to let her sexy ass go. I just hoped Shannon didn't pull this bullshit again, or I would never forgive her, and I'm afraid I might kill her.

Mwah! I woke Shannon up with a kiss on her sexy lips

"Hey bae," Shannon said as she opened her beautiful eyes.

"Hey boo, how you feeling?" I replied as I rubbed her stomach with a big Kool-Aid smile on my face.

"I'm good, a little nauseated."

"I can make you feel better," I said, licking my lips, letting Shannon know I was ready to taste her juices on my tongue.

"Come make feel better then, daddy," Shannon smirked as she started sliding her boy shorts down her thick thighs.

I pulled Shannon's lil' thick ass to the end of the bed, got on my knees, and started to please her. I was eating her pussy like it was my last supper. I moved my tongue around on her clit until I got it super hard and it was sticking out just how I liked it. Then I put my warm lips around her clit and start sucking on it slowly. I could tell it was feeling good the way Shannon was lifting her body in the air up off the bed. She grabbed my head, shoved my face into her dripping pussy, and began moaning loudly.

"Gee! I love you, baby! I promise I love you."

I looked up at Shannon, still slurping on her pussy and said, "I love you too." Then I buried my face back in her pussy. I ate her for at least forty-five minutes. She came so many times, her body was shaking. I pulled out my fat, long monster dick and told Shannon to bend that ass over doggy-style. I slid my dick in her slippery wet pussy and started beating that shit up. I made sure I aimed to please that pussy with every stroke. Shannon started running from this dick and was grabbing the sheets. The harder I hit it, the more she ran.

"Bring that ass here! Stop running and take this dick," I said in an aggressive tone as I gripped her by her hips.

Shannon started creaming all over my dick. I could feel her warm cum gushing out on me. She started throwing her ass back, making it bounce and jiggle on my dick. Shannon knew that drove me crazy. I got to the point I couldn't take it anymore. I nutted all up in her pussy, moaning her name loudly. You can tell I dicked her down good because when I got finished, she stayed in the same position for a while.

TK

I don't know what it is about that nigga Cage, but I'm not feeling him. I got a bad vibe from him. I understand that's Gee's nigga, but all these niggas ain't your friends. I'm going to keep a close eye on Cage. The nigga seems skep to me.

"Hey, boo. I missed you," Kandi said as she walked through the door and greeted me with a kiss.

"I missed you, too. Where you been?"

"Handling business."

"Oh. Come make me feel good," I bit my bottom lip looking at Kandi's lil' short, thick ass.

"Don't start nothing you can't finish," Kandi replied as she pulled her dress off and began to get naked.

Man, Kandi's body was so sexy and petite. She had a round bubble butt, tiny waist, and some nice size breasts. I can't lie, I used to miss that shit when I was in jail. *I beat my meat every night thinking about her lil' sexy ass,* I laughed to myself. *But tonight, I'm about to tear that pussy out the frame.* Kandi walked over to the couch, got on her knees, gripped my dick, and started sucking it.

"Aww shit, that feel good, Kandi."

The more I talked to her, the more she sucked. Kandi's head was the best. No woman had ever sucked or fucked me the way Kandi did. I put my hand on the back of Kandi's head and moved her head up and down. She was slobbering and slurping on that dick so good my toes started to curl. I pushed her head back, letting her know I couldn't take it.

She stared me in my eyes and said, "Take that head," and spit on my dick and started sucking it again. She began to jack my dick and lick it at the same time. She was driving me crazy. Kandi got up, sat on my dick, and commenced to riding it. Her pussy was so wet my dick was drenched. I grabbed her juicy ass cheeks and started slamming her down on my long log.

"Umm shit," Kandi moaned. "Slam me down harder, daddy. I want to feel it in my stomach."

The sound of Kandi's voice made my dick even harder. I stood up, still holding Kandi on my dick. She wrapped her arms around my neck and her legs around my waist. She began to move up and down on my dick. Every time she was about to come down, I slammed her down hard. I wanted her to feel all these inches in her.

After fucking her for a while, I removed her from my dick and laid her on the floor gently. I spread her legs wide open and begin kissing all over her fat shaved pussy. I stuck my tongue deep in her juice box and wiggled it around. Kandi went crazy. Next I turned her over and started hitting it from the back. The way her ass vibrated on my dick made me go hard in that pussy. Before I knew it, I was nutting all on her ass.

When we were finished, we lay there a while. I looked at Kandi and she was fast asleep on the floor. I picked her lil' ass up, carried her to the bedroom and lay her in the bed. I went back down to the living room and started rolling my Kush joint up. I took a hit of the Kush, and started reminiscing about life. Damn, I'd been with Kandi since I was a young boy. I've gotten to watch her blossom from a young lady to a woman. I know I left her and did some time in jail, but I wasn't going back and I was going to make sure of that.

Even though Kandi was in on the robbery with me, I couldn't let her go to jail, so I took the fall for everything. I loved Kandi with all my heart and I was going to do whatever to make us happy. Before I went to jail, I was on some stupid shit. Slanging drugs, robbing niggas, fighting, shooting, clubbing, I did everything a street nigga could do. But doing that bid behind bars did something to me. I realized I'm a grown ass man, so now I had to get on my grown shit.

The whole time I was in jail, Kandi, Gee, and Chaos were the only people who held me down. My own mama didn't even come see me. So, it's only right I pay them back when I get on my feet. While incarcerated, I got my barber's license and a bricklaying certificate. My plan was to get out here and change my life around for the better. When you're in jail, all you can do is think about life and what you're going to do to make it better. But don't get me wrong, the street nigga's still in me, just resting, not dead.

"Aww shit," I said out loud as the fire from my joint dropped on my lap, interrupting my thoughts. I wiped the fire off my pants.

"Damn, I'm tripping." I got up, walked to the kitchen, and poured myself a drink.

"What you doing," Kandi yelled, scaring the shit out of me.

"Man, you scared the shit out of me. I almost beat your ass."

"Boy gone, you wasn't going to do shit," Kandi mushed me in my head and laughed.

"Why you walking around here naked anyway? Put your clothes on before I bend that ass over again," I chuckled and slapped her on her ass.

I love the relationship me and Kandi had, but I still wonder if she was as loyal to me as she claims she was. She swears up and down she didn't fuck around on me, but my sources are telling me differently. I wasn't expecting Kandi to be faithful, I just told her don't let nobody take her heart away from me.

Kandi

Even though TK was locked up for years, I never stopped loving him I held him down the whole time. I made sure I visited him, sent letters, pictures, and kept money on his books. I can't lie, when TK left me and went to jail I was scared. We did so much dirt to people I felt like they were going to try and take me out when TK went away, but I held my own. Everybody knew I stayed strapped, but TK was like my body guard. Anywhere you saw me, you saw him. So, when TK got sent up it seem like the world was on my shoulders. He left me a couple of bricks, so I hustled to make sure he was good.

Even though TK didn't approve of it because he was afraid somebody was going to rob me or kill me for it, I still did it. I lied to TK and told him I got a job working at a bank. Until one day, he had somebody call the bank and ask for me and they said they'd never heard of me. We had a big argument because I lied to him. TK can deal with a lot of shit, but a liar is not one of them. He asked me had I been faithful to him the whole time he was in jail. I told him yeah. I knew I was wrong for lying. I didn't tell him I'd slept with Blaze, because if he finds out, all hell's going to break loose. *But now that I think about it, he might like it,* I laughed to myself.

I knew it was only a matter of time before he found out, so I knew I had to hurry up and tell him before Gee did. TK meant the world to me, and the last thing I wanted to do was lose him because I was lusting over some stripper bitch. Blaze did her thang, don't get me wrong. I even started catching feelings for her. After I found out she was sleeping with Shannon, I had no choice but to cut her off. I was mad at Shannon, but I realized it wasn't her fault. She didn't know, I just wished she would've told me.

Blaze started turning crazy, stalking me, watching my every move, and she was too jealous. Word on the street, Blaze was fucking Gee's ex-girlfriend Amber, but I always had my suspicions about those two hoes. Like the old saying goes, birds of a feather flock together. If Blaze is messing with Amber I can't tell, because she still blowing up my phone and texting me like crazy. I had to let Blaze know I couldn't mess with her because she slept with my best friend and, on top of that, TK was home from jail and that's where my heart is.

I'm not going to lie, I still thought about Blaze and lusted for her from time to time, but I couldn't see myself falling back into her lustful trap. It's obvious Blaze liked eating anybody with a pussy. She went from Shannon to me and possibly Amber, one of the dirtiest hoes in the Atlanta. Blaze was so sexy and her mouth game was off the chain. She could turn a straight woman gay for one night. I'd never been with another woman. But when I got drunk at the strip club that night and got a private dance from Blaze, my pussy instantly started screaming for her touch. Her body was like a goddess, I'd never seen anything like it. When I finally let her taste my juices, I'd never felt anything like it.

I was turned out. I had to have her every night and every day. She even ate my pussy at her job, in the car, on the car, and a lot of other places. *Umm,* I said to myself as I had flash about her kissing all on this pussy and eating it until I squirted all my juices in her mouth.

"Kandi! Kandi," TK yelled, fucking up my thoughts. "What you thinking about," TK said with a puzzled look on his face.

"Nothing."

"Shit, something! I been calling your name you didn't answer," TK replied as he took a sip of his drink.

"You're crazy baby. I wasn't thinking about nothing."

"Yeah okay. Whatever, Kandi."

Dang, I'm slipping, I said to myself. *I'm over here lusting for Blaze while the man I love is standing right here in my face. I got to get myself together before TK thinks I'm messing around on him.*

Cage

"Yeah, let me get two shots of Hennessey," I asked as I sat in the bar in the strip club waiting for Blaze to perform. I felt bad knowing I had to kill a woman, but a nigga killed my mama, so I don't have no mercy for no one.

I sat back, thinking about her death and what it had made me. My sister got adopted after my mama died, so I never met her. But I've been looking for her for years. I wasn't going to stop until I found her.

"Two shots of Henny up," the waitress said.

"Thanks, Ms. Lady. Keep the change."

I waited patiently for this Blaze chick to come out, but everybody was coming out except Blaze. I looked at my Rolex to see what time it was.

Damn, it's a quarter 'til one and she still not out. It must not be her time to die, I said to myself. I took my last shot of Henny and headed toward the door. Before I knew it, the music began to play.

"Coming to the stage is the one and only Blaze and she is blazing," the DJ said over the mic.

I took a seat closer to the stage so I could get a good look at Blaze. I didn't want to make any mistakes. When Blaze came out onto the stage, my heart dropped and my dick got rock hard. The girl was a dime and she knew it. She had an unbelievable body, the type of body you couldn't even explain to your niggas, they would just have to see it.

We made eye contact and she kept her eyes on me. I know Blaze was thinking "he a boss," because I dress like one and act like one. Strippers can smell a nigga with money from a mile away, so I knew Blaze had her eyes on me for a reason. She just didn't know death was sitting right in her face. Blaze began to dance and I had a front row seat. This bitch was so damn sexy I wanted to just fuck the shit out of her right there. I threw her sexy ass a couple of hundreds and headed towards the exit. I looked back as I walked away. Blaze had her eyes on me the whole time.

"I'm tripping. I got to get it together," I said to myself, smoking my Cuban as I sat in my Lexus. I was tripping heavy! It was like love at first sight when I saw Blaze. I think the fact that I haven't had a woman in my life for a long time had me bugging. Shit, I couldn't think of the last time I'd had sex, but my money felt better than pussy. I pulled off, headed back to my spot, and gave Gee a call.

"What up with it, Gee?"

"Nothing much. You handle that,"

"Nah, not yet, but I'm in the process. I need my down payment."

"What we talking"

"Seventy-five thousand and when the job's complete, you can give me the other half."

"Aight, that's cool."

"I'll hit you up some time this week with a time and location."

"Cool."

Blaze

"Amber, I don't know who that fine brother was that had a front row seat, but I was on his ass like white on rice."

"Who you talking about? I seen the same raggedy ass niggas we dance for every night."

"Girl, it was nothing raggedy about this man. He was fine as wine and he looked like a boss."

"Girl, please. Just because a nigga fine and look like a boss don't make him a boss, Blaze."

"I recognize a boss when I see one, trust me."

"Yeah, yeah, whatever, Blaze. See you tomorrow."

"Whatever."

I sat in the dressing room for a while just thinking about life. I loved the strip life, but I was tired of it. I got paid good money and I was addicted to it, but this wasn't the type of life I wanted for myself. I saw myself married with about two kids and living in a nice house on the beach. I noticed since I started stripping I changed who I used to be.

Before I became a dancer, I stayed in Miami, Florida. I was messing with this big-time drug dealer named Jason. I had everything I wanted, but he started to turn abusive. I stayed with him for a while, even after he began to beat me. I loved him so much and I didn't have any family. My mother gave me up when I was little. She was a crack head. She was also schizo. My sister is married. We talked every blue moon, and my brother is locked up in Virginia doing life. I never met him before, but my foster parents used to keep me updated about my siblings when I was younger.

Jason and I did everything together. He's the one who turned me out on females and going to the strip club. I had a threesome with Jason a couple of times with this girl, Tia. She and Jason began to get close and I wasn't feeling that, but I never mentioned it to him. One particular day, Jason was out of town and Tia came over and one thing led to another. Every other time me and Tia had sex Jason was there, but this particular night, he was out of town handling some business.

Tia came over and one thing led to another. We were going hard, she taught me everything I needed to know when it came to having sex with another woman. Her head game was dangerous. I used to be climbing the walls trying to run from her tongue. Tia put on a strap-on and fucked the shit out of me. Jason ended up walking in on us fucking. He acted a damn fool! He beat the hell out of me and Tia, and I haven't seen since.

After that, Jason turned very aggressive, and the drugs he was doing wasn't making it any better. We started to fight every night until I couldn't take it anymore. Jason knew I was about to leave him, so he hired a bodyguard to keep an eye on me. I had to play Jason at his own game. I hired a hitman and got the bodyguard killed. I left town and have not been back to Miami.

Word on the streets of Miami was Jason had a price tag on my head for fifty thousand. Whoever found me had to bring me back to him, and he will handle it from there. I'd been keeping a low profile, but I didn't know how long that was going to last. When I was fifteen I was diagnosed with schizophrenia, just like my crazy ass mother. I made sure I took all my medication, but since I moved to Atlanta, I hadn't had any medicine. I'd been too scared Jason would find me.

I'd been hiding in Atlanta for the last year and a half, trying to stack this money so I could move far, far away. Even though now, I'm not leaving Atlanta until I get what belonged to me, which was Shannon. When I first saw Shannon I wanted her and when I finally got her, I fell deep in love with her. At first it was a lust thing, but as we spent more time around each other, I fell deeper for her.

I know Shannon's with Gee, but I can't seem to keep her off my mind. I have flashbacks of me pleasing her all the time. If I can't have Shannon, nobody can. I don't regret shooting her, either. I kind of wished she would've died so I wouldn't be fighting for her. I was just letting everything cool down before I made my next move. Shannon could pretend she doesn't want me, but I know she does and I'm going to put up a fight to get her. Kandi, on the other hand… I have some feeling for Kandi, but she doesn't compare to Shannon. Kandi was just something do at first, but I started feeling her. I still call her and text her, but she's been ignoring me lately.

Gee

"How you feeling, Shannon? Come here, let me kiss on your stomach."

"I'm okay. I got something you can kiss on, Gee."

"Shit, let me kiss that too."

"You so nasty."

"Nasty for you only, Shannon. You hungry? You want some breakfast?"

"Yes, I'm starving, Gee."

"You want some sausage?" Gee laughed, grabbing his hard, fat twelve-inch dick.

"Ha-ha, you play too much."

"I'm just playing. Get dressed, we going to breakfast."

"Okay."

Things between me and Shannon were starting to be better than ever, but I still had a question in my heart about her. She did cheat with another woman. *Damn, what was I slipping on?* I questioned myself. *I know I put it down and I eat the shit out of Shannon's pussy, but I don't know if that's enough.*

She went to a woman for a reason and that's what really hurt me. What could that bitch do that I couldn't? I know I put it down in the bedroom, but I find myself wondering what Blaze did to Shannon to make her cheat on me. I'm praying to God Shannon doesn't fuck up again because I know deep, deep down in my soul I'd kill Shannon with no hesitation and that's on my life.

She claimed Blaze had been calling and playing on her phone. I told Shannon to get her number changed, but she didn't do it yet. It had me wondering if she was still talking to this chick or if she loved the attention. I'm praying to God Shannon doesn't betray me again because if she does it's going to get ugly.

"I'm ready, baby," Shannon said, standing there with a lil' pudge in her stomach. Every time I looked at Shannon, my heart skipped a beat. Knowing that she was carrying my child inside of her made me love her even more.

"Gee, I'm ready. You hear me? I'm ready."

"My bad baby, I'm just admiring your sexy ass. I don't never want to lose you at all."

"You don't never have to worry about that, Gee. I told you I want you and only you."

A part of my heart wanted to believe Shannon, but the other part didn't.

"I believe you, Shannon."

Really, I didn't. I just couldn't t tell her that.

Shannon

I can't wait to marry Gee, I said to myself. Even though I hurt this man to the fullest, I regret every minute of it.

Sometimes I think Gee has lost his faith in us, but I try every day to keep him happy. I love him, and I'm not letting anyone, I mean anyone, come between that again. Blaze had been calling and texting me lately, throwing all types of threats. I think something is seriously wrong with this bitch. I told her I didn't want anything to do with her, but she continued to call and text me. She told me if she couldn't have me, nobody could and I knew she wasn't playing.

I told Gee she was hitting me up. He told me to get my number changed, but I didn't, for what reason I don't even know. Sometimes I did think about me and Blaze having sex, but I got that thought out my mind real fast. I don't think I can ever lust for Blaze or any other woman again. Not only did I hurt myself, I hurt others that were around me too. I could've gotten Gee, Chaos, Kandi, Maria, and myself killed because I was selfish and I was only thinking about what I wanted. I had a long talk with my brother Chaos. I still wanted him to take Blaze out because I knew she wasn't about to give up. Chaos told me whenever I was ready give him the word, but I wasn't trying to put fuel to the fire just yet.

"Shannon," Gee said in a kind of aggressive voice, interfering with my thoughts.

"Yes?"

"Why you didn't get your number changed yet? What's the problem?"

"Oh, I forgot. I'll do it soon as I get home."

"Don't forget this time," Gee responded.

"Okay."

Gee and I continued to eat breakfast. I could tell the whole time something was on Gee's mind. I asked Gee numerous times if something was bothering him, but he kept telling me nothing.

TK

"Kandi, you want to hit up the strip club tonight for old time's sake? I heard Dream Girls be popping, bae."

"Umm, I don't know, TK. I'm tired."

"Man, get your ass up and get dressed. I don't want to hear that shit. When I was in jail you didn't have a problem with going."

"Okay, I'll go."

Kandi started getting dressed, taking her sweet time like she didn't want to go. I wasn't really a club nigga, but I just wanted to see some strippers. Back in the day before I got locked up, me and Kandi stayed hitting up the strip clubs. Now that I'm out, Kandi was acting brand new. When I was in jail, she couldn't keep her ass out the strip club. I rolled up as I waited for Kandi to get dressed.

"Damn, what's taking you so long to get dressed," I shouted.

"Here I come now."

When Kandi came down, she was looking fine as ever. She had on some black jeans that hugged every inch of her hips and ass, a half shirt, and some red bottom heels. The way those jeans gripped her petite curves had me wanting to take her back upstairs.

"I'm ready, TK."

"Damn, me too," I replied in a sarcastic way, rubbing my dick.

"Don't start nothing I'll have to finish."

"Girl, you better stop talking like that 'fore I beat that pussy like you stole something," I said looking at Kandi in a sexual manner.

"Ha-Ha, bring your ass on boy."

We arrived at Dream Girls and it was packed. The line was outrageous. Thank God I had pull. Me and Kandi walked in and got a couple of drinks. I was feeling good and my eyes were super low from smoking that killa. We sat right by the stage where we could see everything. Kandi was throwing all the dancers money. She even paid one to give me a lap dance. We were enjoying our night until the next dancer that came out was Blaze.

"Man, is that the bitch that shot Gee and Shannon?"

"Umm, yeah," Kandi answered with a shaky voice. For some reason, Kandi looked edgy to me. I couldn't blame her though, she shot her best friend.

"What's wrong with you, baby? Why you look uneasy?"

"It's nothing TK, I just don't like that bitch. Can we leave now?"

"Hell nah, I'm not about to let no stripper bitch ruin our night."

I don't know what the hell was up with Kandi, but something wasn't right. I understood she was uncomfortable when Blaze came out. Who can blame her, though? She wasn't the only one uncomfortable. I was ready to beat the shit out of Blaze, but I wasn't going back to jail for her, and Gee already got a hit on her ass anyway. Boy, that lil' bitch was fine, though. *But not finer than my baby,* I thought to myself.

I noticed when Blaze came out, Kandi stopped throwing money and she wasn't trying to look her way. I saw that Blaze kept looking over at Kandi. Something felt off, but I couldn't put my finger on it. Blaze walked off the stage and started walking toward some nigga dressed like a lawyer. The dude she was dancing for looked familiar, but I was so high and drunk I couldn't remember where I knew him from. I put my focus on the other stripper that was dancing. I looked over at Kandi and caught her and Blaze making eye contact. *Something's not right,* I thought to myself. The look Blaze was giving Kandi was not acceptable, but I shook that shit off.

Kandi

I'm so ready to go, I said to myself. I was feeling uncomfortable and out of place. Blaze was giving me a seductive look and I could've sworn TK saw it. Blaze was so damn ignorant she didn't care who she hurt as long as she got what she wanted. I tried my best not to give Blaze any eye contact because I didn't want TK having any kind of skepticism about us. Blaze was dancing on some fine looking brother. You could tell he was a boss and he was about his business. She was dancing on him, but she was staring at me.

What Blaze and I had is now gone, and I didn't want it back at all. I had to admit, I had love for her, but she disrespected to the fullest. On top of that, she let Chaos smash her and she didn't even know him. I went to college with Blaze years ago, so I didn't know much about her. What I did know was something's not right about her. In college, she was one of those quiet girls. You know, the quiet ones that didn't say much until you got to know them. Blaze and I hung out sometimes, but she never made a pass at me. But I know one thing, I was going to find out what's going on in that little sick bitch's head. She better hope I didn't kill her ass. Blaze thought I didn't see the way she was looking while she gave her lap dance. She was trying to get me caught up and it wasn't going to work. I'd rip her heart out her chest and feed it to a Pitbull before I allowed her to break me and TK up with her stupidity.

"TK baby, I'll be right back. I'm about to grab me another drink," I whispered in TK's ear as I got out my seat.

"Baby, get me a shot of whatever while you there," TK replied with his words slurring as he smacked my ass when I walked off. I looked at TK, gave him a grin, and continued walking.

I could feel Blaze burning a hole in my ass as I walked up to the bar.

"Let me get a strawberry daiquiri and a shot of Goose," I yelled so the bartender could hear me. After waiting for about ten minutes, I finally received our drinks. I began making my way back to my seat, and to my surprise, Blaze was over there giving TK the twerk of his life. I couldn't even believe TK let her touch him after he knew what she did to Shannon and Gee. TK was over the limit drunk. My first instinct was to smack fire out her ass, but I had to rethink my mindset. I set my drink down on the table and handed TK his drink.

"I see you enjoying this lap dance, TK."

"Baby, you tripping. It's just a dance," TK said with a smile on his face, looking drunk as fuck.

Blaze sat down on his lap with her back towards him and started grinding on him slowly. I was burning flames in the inside. I was ready to murder this bitch. It was only a matter of time before I beat the brakes off her ass.

"TK get up, let's go now before I act a fool in Dream Girls. Won't none of these hoes have a dream anymore."

"Man, I just threw this bitch my money. I'm going to get my money's worth," TK replied.

Blaze gave TK a crazy look because he called her bitch, then she kept dancing. Blaze knew she was pissing me off. She got off TK, turned around, and sat back down on his lap. This time they were sitting face-to-face. Blaze laid back, opened her legs real wide, and started popping her pussy in his face. Before I knew it, I grabbed my drink and tossed it in Blaze's face. TK pushed Blaze off of him and got up.

"Boo, you tripping. What's wrong with you?" TK asked, holding me back so I couldn't demolish Blaze.

Blaze got off the floor and ran up to me.

"Let that bitch go," Blaze yelled, trying to swing over TK.

I pushed TK out of the way. The next thing you know, Blaze had me by my hair and swung me on the floor. I got up and ran up to Blaze.

"What's up, bitch," I yelled and punched that hoe dead in her mouth. I looked at Blaze and her mouth was leaking. I grabbed her hair with both hands and made her face meet my knee. I did this repeatedly. I felt myself getting snatched up by some big security guard.

"My nigga, put my girl down before I destroy your big ass," TK shouted from across the room, while several people held him back.

The security guard escorted TK and I out the building. I saw Blaze kick her heels off and start running toward me, but security caught her before she could get near me.

"Bitch, this ain't over, Kandi," Blaze shouted as I exited.

Blaze

"Damn, ma, you okay?" the brother I was giving a lap dance to earlier said.

"Get the fuck out my face. I'm good." I was so mad I didn't want anybody speaking to me.

"I guess I can accept the fact that you mad right now, so I'm going to let that slide, lil' mama."

"You have no choice," I replied, then walked away and went to my dressing room to get dressed so I could go home. I got finished getting myself together, then I left and headed home. As soon as I arrived at my house, I took a shower, rolled up a fat ass joint, and poured me up a drink. *Damn,* I thought to myself, *I miss Shannon's sexy ass.*

Every time she crossed my mind, my pussy got wet. I could taste her without even seeing her. I grabbed my cell phone and gave Shannon a call, but she didn't answer. She just didn't know I was on her ass. I wasn't letting her go, I loved her and I needed her in my life. A sudden low knock on my door disturbed my thoughts. *Who the hell could be at my door this time of night?*

I got up to open the door. A man was standing there with a dozen roses, looking good as ever.

"Okay that's creepy. How do you know where I live?" I asked with a puzzled look on my face.

"I know everything, lil' mama, I'm the man around town. Can I come in?"

"Hell naw, nigga, I don't know you. I don't even know your name," I shouted and tried to shut the door, but he blocked it with his foot.

He chuckled and responded, "You can get to know me. Just give me a minute of your time and then you can put me out."

I looked him up and down, then finally let him in.

"Damn, you looking good."

"Nigga, I got on a robe. Anyway, what is your name?"

He got quiet for a minute, then finally answered, "My name Cage."

"Nice to meet you, Cage. Would you like a drink?"

"Sure, but I really would like you."

I looked at him with a fake grin, thinking to myself, *Damn, he is fine. I wouldn't mind sitting on that dick, it's been a while since I got fucked good.*

"Can I get a private dance?" Cage asked, holding a stack of money. It had to be at least a thousand dollars and a bitch like me was not turning down any money.

"I knew you was feeling me when I was giving you a lap dance."

"Let me feel you now, sexy."

I began walking over to my radio, turned on some slow jam music, and lit my joint back up. I took three long puffs and put it out.

I untied my robe and let drop to my feet. Cage's face was astonished. I guess he wasn't expecting me to be butt ass naked. I started walking over to Cage with a seductive look in my eyes. I stood in front of him and began to caress my breast. I rubbed my hand from my breast to my pussy, rubbing on my clit until I was dripping wet. Cage threw a couple of hundreds at me. I was going to make sure I got every last one of those hundred dollar bills out of him. I told him hold on I'd be right back. I went to my room, grabbed some peach body oil, and handed it to Cage. I laid down in front of him on the floor, doggy style. Cage scooted to the end of the chair, making sure he could reach my ass, and began pouring the oil on my ass.

"Umm umm umm, ma! Damn you sexy."

I reached my hand back and rubbed the oil in as Cage poured it on my round, fat ass. By this time, my pussy was dripping wet. He rubbed the oil in and commenced to massage my ass. Next thing I knew, he was kissing on my ass cheeks and biting them. Cage got up and started taking off his clothes, but not before he made it rain on me with the rest of his money.

I got up to join Cage and help him come out of his expensive clothing. I unbuckled his pants and slid them off, along with his boxers. Before I knew it, Cage's dick was in my mouth. He had one of those dicks, you know the ones that are long, fat, thick, smooth and when you see it, you just want to suck it. When I dropped his boxers, my mouth watered instantly.

I spit on his dick and jacked it, repeating this step several times. Cage gripped the back of my hair and motioned my head back and forth. I looked up at him to see his reaction and we made eye contact. I couldn't take my eyes off him and he damn sure couldn't take his eyes off me.

After sucking his dick for about twenty minutes, I got up and started kissing Cage's neck. I was so drunk and high it had me on some freaky shit. Cage picked me up, wrapped my legs around his waistline, and started walking over to the wall. My back was against the wall while he stuck himself deep in my pussy. Cage was fucking me so good and rough I immediately started creaming all over his dick. He laid down on the floor, still holding me, and sat me on his face. When I say he ate my mind, spirit, and soul out my body, he did just that.

"Ooh shit," I moaned. As I rode his face, my pussy was drowning him. I could tell by the way he came up for air and then dove his face back in. I began to cum again and again. Cage grabbed me and threw me over doggy style and dug deeply into my ocean of love.

Cage

Damn, she so sexy, I said to myself as I fucked the shit out of her. I was fucking her so good we ended up where we started, in front of the chair on the floor. She didn't know this was the last dick she would feel inside of her because, after I fucked her, my plans were to take her ass out. *Man, she shole do know how to work that ass, though. I bet if she knew she was about to have a bullet in back of her head, she wouldn't be fucking me like that,* I chuckled to myself.

I gripped her hips and started grinding that pussy from the back. She kept running from this dick, but I made her take it. I couldn't front, she was handling this pole like a pro for a while and I was loving it. She had some fire ass pussy, the type of pussy that would make you fall in love soon as you entered it.

I couldn't deny it, her pussy almost had me gone, but I had to stick to my guns. I had a job to do. I continued to hit that ass from the back as I reach under my pants where my pistol was. I resumed pleasing her slippery wet pussy as I slowly slid the gun from under my clothes. Before I could pull the pistol all the way out, she did the most. She squirted all on my dick. It felt like the Niagara Falls. I got weak in my knees.

"Awww fuck Blaze," I screamed out loud, dropping my pistol out my hand back under my pants. *That shit felt so good I damn near shot myself,* I laughed on the inside.

She then turned around and sucked my dick until I busted all on her face. She even kissed the head of my dick when she finished. Afterward, I sat there speechless. This girl is the bomb. I think I'm turned out. I snapped out of my thoughts quickly.

"You got to give me that dick again soon," Blaze said as she got her sexy, naked body off the floor and lit up her joint. She sat down on the couch. I joined her and put on my clothes. She told me to take down her number, we talked for a while, and then I headed out.

"Don't be a stranger," Blaze said as I walked out the door.

I gave Blaze a grimy smile and replied, "Trust me, I won't."

I made it to my car and got in.

"Fuck! Fuck! Fuck!" I yelled, hitting the steering wheel. "I'm fucking tripping! I can't let her take me off my game," I yelled.

I grabbed my Cuban out of the ash tray and pulled off. I couldn't believe the connection between Blaze and I. It was unbelievable. I fired up my cigar and all I can do was have flashbacks of me and Blaze going hard. My dick got hard and I was ready to turn around and go fuck her again.

Gee

My phone woke me up the next morning. It was Cage asking me to meet him over at the hotel he was residing in at noon. I got up, ate breakfast, and put my shit on. That phone call made my day. Just to know I was a step closer to Blaze's death made me even happier. I arrived at the hotel where Cage was residing. When I approach the door, I did the knock Cage asked me to do.

"What up, brah?"

"What's good boss," I replied to Cage.

"Shit, but this money," Cage chuckled, walked over to the table, and took a seat.

"I feel you on that, but here goes your money, my nigga. Instead of half, the whole fifteen thousand is in the bag. I need this this bitch dead in the next seventy-two hours," I said, throwing the duffle bag on the table.

"Look I can't promise she going to be dead in the next seventy-two hours. But I can promise she will be dead, and that's my word."

"As long as that bitch in her grave, I'm a happy camper, and that's real shit."

"That's if they find her body. I might dump that bitch in somebody river."

We both fell out laughing.

Cage poured us up a shot, "I would like to propose a toast to the dead bitch walking," he said sarcastically with an evil grin on his face. We both laugh so hard I almost pissed on myself.

"Cheers to the dead bitch walking and may she rest in peace."

We hit our shot glasses together and took the Henny to the face. My phone began to ring. It was Shannon.

"What's up, bae?"

"Nothing. Where you at, Gee?"

"On my way home in a minute. I had to go handle some business."

"Okay, can you stop and get me some McDonald's, please! I'm craving it and I need it now!"

"Okay baby, calm down. I got you, don't kill me over a fucking burger," I responded sarcastically.

"Shut up Gee, before I bite you."

"If anything, I'm going to be doing the biting."

"Whatever. Go get my Big Mac meal, ten piece nuggets, and two apple pies. Oh, don't forget my large Ice Tea."

"Dayum baby, you playing, right?" I reacted with a confused face.

"Hell naw I'm not playing. Do it sound like I'm playing? Huh? Huh?"

"Calm down, I'm just playing," I laughed out loud. "Shan, you're crazy, man."

"Whatever. I got to go. Somebody at the door."

"Where Chaos at? Have him to answer it."

"Yes, he went to get something to eat."

"Man, I told that nigga not to leave your side. Okay, I will be there shortly."

"Okay."

"Ahy Cage, I'm gon' holla at you soon, my nigga. My lady need me."

"Cool. I'll be at you Gee."

I hopped in my car and headed to McDonalds.

Shannon

"Who is it, damn?"

No one replied.

"Who the hell is it?" I yelled, swinging the door open aggressively, but no one was there.

I looked to the right to see a brick in my car window and Blaze at the end of my driveway, sitting in her car. I stepped out the door and she sped off quickly. I ran back in the house and grabbed my cell phone.

"So, these the type of games you want to play, you trifling bitch," I yelled through the receiver of my cell phone.

"Shannon, baby, it's a pleasure to hear your voice. I been waiting on your call," Blaze said sarcastically.

"You think this shit funny, Blaze? Fuck you!"

"That's what I want you to do, but you chose Gee over me. Remember?"

"You know what Blaze, Blake, whatever your name is. Bitch, you lucky I'm pregnant you psychotic bitch!"

"Ha-ha psychotic, you got that right," Blaze laughed out loud.

"Bitch get off my line," I said, disconnecting our call.

"Ooooohhhhhh, I hate this bitch," I shouted as tears began to flow down my face.

I was so ready to load my gun up and light her ass up with every bullet I had. Blaze was getting out of hand. Not only did she shoot me, Gee, and almost cause harm to our baby, now the hoe was showing up to our house. No, I'm not having it. The bitch had to die as soon as possible. I wouldn't let her destroy my home.

"Aww shit! Oh my God!" I fell to my knees, holding my stomach as sharp cramps went through it. I could barely move. I gained the strength to call Gee, but before I could press the call button, he burst through the door.

"Shannon, baby, you okay? Somebody busted out your windows," Gee screamed in concern, only to find me on the floor holding my stomach. He ran over, picked me up off the floor, and laid me on the couch.

"No. My stomach hurts bad, Gee. Call 911!"

"Who did this to you? Did Blaze do this shit?" Gee asked as tears ran down his face.

"She bust out the car windows and left, but she didn't touch me."

Gee ran, opened the house door and car door, then picked me up off the couch and carried me to his car. I laid in the back seat of the car as Gee hit a hundred to the hospital. *If I lose my baby I'm going to murder Blaze,* I thought.

Blaze

I loved Shannon and I was going to do whatever it took to get her attention, even if that meant stalking her ass. I busted her car windows out just to get her attention. A*t least I got the call I was waiting on,* I snickered.

But since Shannon won't come to me, I was going to make her come to me. I called up my boy O Dog. He's a ruthless nigga from the Bronx, but he stays here in Atlanta, GA.

"What up, O Dog?"

"Blaze, my nigga! What's up, girl? Where yo' ass been at, ma?"

"Laying low and getting money."

"I feel that. So, what's up?"

"I need you to kidnap this bitch for me."

O Dog laughed, "What you want for real, Blaze?"

"I'm serious. I'm not laughing."

"You know it's going to cost you, right?"

"I know. How much we talking, O Dog?"

"Ten bands."

"Ten bands? Shit, that's kind of steep, but I got you."

"Damn, what this bitch do to you?"

"I will explain everything tomorrow. Meet me at the strip club I work at around seven."

"Cool."

Shannon wanted to play hard to get but she just didn't know she good as got. On the other hand, I was kind of feeling Cage's sexy ass. The sex was off the hook and he'd been on my mind heavy. He'd been calling me all day. He made me smile and the conversation we had on the phone, you would've thought we'd known each other forever. I spent my day trying to find my brother in prison. I needed to find him ASAP. I was feeling lonely and out here all by my damn self. At least if I found him, I could find out more about my family. After doing my research, I found out that my brother Derrick had been out of jail for years and he lived somewhere in GA. I lucked up, now I had to do some more searching.

Cage

Blaze's fine ass had been on my mind since I left her crib. The visions I got in my head of when I was fucking her made my dick hard immediately. I snapped out of my thoughts. I loved the way she sucked me and fucked me. Damn, it's got to be a crime to look that good and fuck that good. *Too bad all that sexiness would go to waste soon,* I chuckled to myself.

I had a plan. I just hoped everything went as planned. If I could get Blaze wrapped around my finger and for her to trust me, this murder would be perfect. I called Blaze up and spit some fire game in her ear. Before I hung up, she was telling me to come over before she went to work. I know I'm wrong for fucking Blaze but she's the shit. Unfortunately, she still had to die.

I arrived at Blaze's house about five. I approached the door. Before I could even knock, Blaze opened the door and was standing there butt ass naked. My dick got so hard I was ready to fuck Blaze's brains out, and that's exactly what I was about to do. Blaze instantaneously started ripping my clothes off and pushed me against the wall. She started sucking my dick like it was a popsicle on a summer day and she couldn't wait to quench her thirst. I got weak in the knees, her head game was the truth.

I moved Blaze off of my dick and told her to do a handstand and spread her legs like the letter V. She did just that. I put my face between her legs and started eating her pussy up like I'd missed a couple of meals. I twirled my tongue around her clit. I could feel Blaze's body starting to vibrate. She released her waterfall all over my face.

Blaze looked at me, bit her lip, then said, "Come fuck me."

I grabbed her up from her handstand and told her to make her hands touch her toes. I inserted my long, fat log into her ocean of love as I gripped both cheeks. I then began to cram all of me into her slowly. Blaze began to moan out of control.

"Ooh Cage! This dick the truth! Fuck me harder." The words rolling off Blaze's lips made me even hornier.

"Be careful what you ask for," I replied. I began to fuck Blaze roughly, making sure she felt every inch that I had to offer. Blaze was taking that dick like a champ. I position her body doggy style and gave her the business. She was squirting uncontrollably. I could feel her pussy muscles squeezing my dick. I began to demolish Blaze's pussy, constantly brutalizing her pussy from the back. She began to run from it. I grabbed her back and slammed her on my dick. She started throwing that ass back and before I knew it, I was nutting all in her.

"Damn," I said as I got up. Blaze was still laying in the position I left her in, breathing heavily. I laughed out loud.

"You good down there?"

"Huh? Yeah, I'm good. You just fucked the shit out of me. I knew from Blaze's reaction I had her right where I wanted her: sprung.

TK

Kandi and I rushed over to the hospital after we heard that Shannon was admitted. When we walked in, Chaos and Gee were there. I was over the limit mad that Blaze kept messing with Shannon.

"TK, let me holler at you and Chaos outside the room real quick." I already knew what Gee was on, the look in his eyes told it all.

"Look, y'all know I already hired a hitman for Blaze, but to make his job easier. I need y'all to go down to the club and kidnap that bitch, *tonight*."

"Gee, I don't think that's a good idea, brah. I mean you already paid that nigga, let him handle that shit," I said.

"I feel where you coming from, TK, but I also feel where Gee coming from. I'm down for whatever, and right about now I'm ready to do whatever to this trick." Chaos grabbed his waist and gripped the handle of his pistol.

"Man alright, I'll go with you Chaos, but nigga I'm not going to jail for nobody."

"Bet," Gee said and shook our hands.

"Come on, we need to be heading out then," Chaos said, happily.

I'd never seen a nigga so happy to do some bullshit in my life. That's how you knew Chaos was crazy. We headed out to the strip club. I told Gee to make sure Kandi got home safe. I couldn't let her know what I was going to do because she would be pissed and I didn't feel like hearing her damn mouth. When we pulled up to the club, it was packed as hell. That was a good thing because nobody should notice us in the building and they would be too busy watching the strippers anyway. I lit up my Kush and took it to the head.

"God, what I'm getting myself into? Please protect me and Chaos." I really wasn't feeling this scheme at all. When we got in the club, we went straight to the bar I order me and Chaos a drink.

"Chaos brah, you think we should do this shit?"

"You think we should do this shit? Hell yeah," Chaos mocked me as he laughed.

"TK, stop acting like a bitch."

"Naw nigga, ain't no bitch in my blood. Fuck you mean?"

"Calm down nigga, I'm just fucking playing."

"Don't play with me like that Chaos, brah," I took my drink to the face.

We talked for at least thirty minutes before Blaze came out. When she did, the crowd went crazy.

"Umm umm, she fine. I see why Shannon let her taste her," Chaos said.

Blaze was dancing on some chick, then she walked over to the same nigga I'd seen her dancing with when I was with Kandi. The nigga looked so familiar but I still couldn't figure out where I knew him from.

"Chaos, you know that nigga Blaze dancing on?"

"Naw. He looks familiar as hell though," Chaos replied.

I was not going to rest until I figure out where I'd seen this nigga at.

"Bartender, give me a shot of Remy." I receive my shot and drank it ASAP. You could tell Blaze knew this nigga from how they were acting. She was whispering all in his ear, you could tell they was having a conversation. A good one, too. When Blaze began to walk away, he smacked her on her ass. She looked back and smiled.

Then it dawned on me! The nigga Blaze was dancing all on was Cage. I knew that nigga was skep. I hit up Gee immediately to let him know what I'd seen, but he wasn't convinced. He said he needed some more evidence. He told me to cancel the plan and follow Blaze home to see if the nigga popped up. I explained to Chaos what was going on as we headed to my ride. He was ready to kill Blaze and Cage on spot.

Kandi

"Where the fuck you at?" I yelled as soon as TK picked up the phone.

"I'm on a mission, baby, I will be there soon."

"Mission? Mission? What type of mission you on? You with some bitch?"

"Hell naw, I'm with Chaos."

"Oh, you better be, and where y'all at?"

"I will explain it to you when I get there, baby. I promise"

"Whatever," I said and hung up the phone.

TK must think I'm a damn fool. Anytime he's with Chaos there's always some shit in the game. Chaos is crazy, trigger happy, and doesn't care who he hurts. I rolled up a fat ass joint and put on some music to relax my mind. I didn't know what TK and Chaos were up to, but I got a bad feeling about this.

I sat there thinking for a couple of hours, then it came to me that they were on their way to Blaze's house. That's why they had Gee drop me off. These motherfuckers thought they were slick. If they knew Blaze like I did, they would be careful. But on the other hand, Blaze better be careful. I ran upstairs to my bedroom and changed my clothes just in case I had to kick somebody's ass. I opened the drawer on my nightstand where my pistol was located and made sure it was fully loaded. I ran downstairs, grabbed my car keys off the kitchen table, and jumped in my ride.

Chaos

"Man, brah, I'm tired of sitting in this parking lot waiting on this bitch. I'm not no private detective. I don't even like the police and this nigga got us doing some police work." I grabbed my cell phone out my pocket and began to text Gee.

"Nigga chill, out and hit this Kush." TK hit the joint and handed it to me.

"Why we can't just go in there and kidnap Blake and beat the shit out of her then kill this lame ass nigga Cage?" I said with a serious ass attitude.

"Nigga, because I told you I'm not going to jail for you or nobody else," TK pointed his finger at me.

"Blaze is sexy as hell though." I laughed out loud. "I fucked her thick ass, too."

"Damn, you fucked Blaze, too?"

"Hell yeah I did! Who didn't fuck her nasty ass?" I hit the Kush and handed it back to TK.

"Nigga, I didn't fuck her nasty ass! That's who!"

"Shit, might as well say you did. Shit, Kandi fucked her."

"What the fuck you just say?"

"I said Kandi fucked her. You ain't know?"

"Hell naw! I'm about to beat Kandi's ass. She got me fucked up! Acting like she hate that bitch so much and she fucked her." TK grabbed his phone and started scrolling down his call list to dial Kandi.

"Aww shit, I thought you knew, my G," I said.

"Man, hang up the phone. There go that nigga Cage coming out now." TK hung up with an angry look on his face. "Look, there go that hoe Blaze, too."

Blaze walked over to her car and got in. Cage had pulled off before us. We followed Blaze, keeping a good distance from her. She made a couple of stops before she went home. She came out somebody's house carrying a white envelope. When she finally arrived home, Cage was sitting in his car in front of her house.

"Chaos, take a picture."

"Ahy, I told you I'm not no fucking detective. I'm not taking no pictures."

"Nigga, just take the pictures!"

"Alright nigga, damn."

I took the pictures as we sat and watched Blaze and Cage enter the house.

Blaze

I got a phone call earlier from a resource saying they had some pictures and information for me about my brother. As soon as I got off work, I headed over to pick this information up. I couldn't wait to get home to open this. When I pull up at home I seen Cage waiting for me my pussy got drench ASAP. I got out of the car and started switching hard as hell to my door. I knew Cage was watching me through that dark ass tint. I heard his door shut when I walked into my house, so I left it open for him.

"Umm, you looking good baby," Cage said grabbing his dick, showing me that it was hard and ready.

"You look even better," I replied.

"What you got in that envelope," Cage asked.

"Nothing, just some important info I been waiting on."

"Oh. Get naked," Cage chuckled.

"You don't have to tell me twice," I replied and started taking off my shirt and jeans.

I didn't know what it was about Cage but he did something to me. He'd actually been taking my mind off Shannon a little, but I still craved her. Cage grabbed my hand and walked me to my bedroom. He told me to lay on my stomach. He began to massage my back and ass cheeks, he kept smacking my ass. Cage then began to kiss on my ass cheeks and bite them. He picked me up off the bed, turned my body upside down, holding me by my hips. My face was directly in front of his long, hard penis. He wrapped my leg around his neck and inserted his tongue into my pussy hole. We were doing a sixty-nine standing up. I spit saliva all over his dick and used my right hand to play with his balls.

"Man you sucking the shit out my dick," Cage said as he lifted his face out of my pussy and dove back in.

We were all into it, I had Cage going crazy and vice versa. Cage threw me down on the bed roughly and pulled me all the way to the edge. He got on his knees and gave me the greatest head ever. I was moaning and groaning, I moved up and down on his face, cumming numerous times. Every time I came, my clit was so sensitive I didn't want Cage to even touch it anymore. But it felt so good I couldn't even stop him. the attraction between me and him was unbelievable. After that, he told me to stand up so he could hit me from the back, leaning over the bed. He slid his dick into my slick wetness. I gripped the sheets because I could feel every inch of his dick in my stomach. He clutched my hips tightly, fucking me crudely from the back.

"Umm, that dick is good! Hit it harder." Cage gripped my hips even tighter, beating the pussy like there was no tomorrow.

"Damn this ass look good. I love the way that shit jiggle," he said, stroking my pussy with his long dick.

"I'm about to nut baby, come suck this dick."

I turned around, got on my knees, and caught every drip of Cage's nut on my tongue. I slapped his dick on my tongue and kissed every inch of it. I walked into the bathroom to get myself together quickly. I was so anxious to open that envelope. I grabbed my silk Chanel robe off the back of the bathroom door, covered my naked body, and walked into the living room. Cage was sitting on the couch with everything on except his shirt. I glanced over at his sexy body. I grabbed the envelope off the table and sat on the sofa across from Cage. I started ripping the envelope open. I had the biggest smile on my face.

"You ripping that open like it's a damn Christmas present," Cage laughed.

"Ha-ha shut up."

I grabbed some pictures out and start looking at them. I couldn't believe my eyes. My heart was pounding tremendously. I began to read the note that was attached to one of the pictures.

Dear Blake, here are some pictures and a phone number for your brother. This is all the info I have for now. His name is Derick C Jonson, he goes by the name Cage. I hope this is helpful.

My breath left my body and the pictures and note fell from my hand.

"What the fuck," Cage said, pulling his gun out.

"Wait, wait! Let me explain Cage."

"Bitch get to explaining! Why the fuck you got pictures of me, bitch? You got somebody watching me? Huh? Huh?" Cage pointed the gun at me.

"No! No, it's not that"

"Bitch you better talk and make it quick!" Cage cocked his gun back aiming it at me, with rage in his eyes.

"Okay look, I been looking for my brother. I have not seen him in years."

"Bitch, what that got to do with me?" he asked, still aiming his gun directly towards my face.

"You're my brother," I said sadly with tears flowing down my face.

TK

I can't believe Kandi would keep a secret from me like that after all we'd been through. My feelings were hurt and I was ready to beat Kandi's ass. Luckily, I was trying to be a changed man because the TK five years ago would 've beat Kandi and Blaze's asses, but she still had it coming.

My phone started to ring, throwing my thoughts off.

"Yeah."

"Where y'all niggas at?" I put the phone on speaker so Chaos could hear what Gee had to say.

"What up, Gee? I was just about to call you. We over here in front of Blaze's house and that nigga Cage in there, too."

"Man, what! What? This nigga got my money and ain't doing his job? Oh we got a big problem."

"I got pictures of the nigga too, Gee. Let me just go kill both of they asses," Chaos shouted.

"Naw, I got a better plan than that," Gee replied.

"So, what's the plan," I asked.

"Let me think. For now, just watch the house. I'll call y'all back soon, they releasing Shannon so I have to take her home."

"That's what's up. We waiting."

"Aight."

"Man, fuck this," Chaos said and got out the door.

"Get your hot ass in the car," I said in a hostile, but low voice.

This was exactly why I don't like doing shit with his hot ass. He can't control his fucking temper. I grabbed my chrome nine from under the seat, got out the car, and followed Chaos to tell him to come on. By the time I got to him, his ass was on Blaze's doorstep. *Fuck, man, he tripping. This exactly why I don't take this nigga nowhere,* I thought to myself.

"Chaos, get your dumb ass down here." He ignored me as he removed his gun out of its holster.

"Fuck you, Chaos. I'm out. I told yo' ass I'm not going to jail for none of y'all."

"TK, come listen to this shit."

I didn't know if I should turn back around or keep it moving, but the look on Chaos' face was disturbing. I turned around, holding my gun close to me, cocked and ready. As I approached the porch, I could hear Blaze and Cage arguing. I put my ear close to the door so I could hear what the conflict was about. Then I noticed somebody creeping up in all black. I tapped Chaos and nodded my head in the direction of this unknown person. We both aimed our pistols in that direction.

Shannon

After the doctor released me from the hospital I was placed on bedrest. I was so sick of being on bedrest. It felt like I'd just gotten off bedrest from being shot. When I came home, Gee helped me upstairs to the bedroom and helped me put on my pajamas. Gee kissed me on my forehead and told me he had to make a run to the store and he would be back shortly. I was so exhausted by the time Gee left, I was passed out. I got woke up to Gee rubbing his hand up my thigh.

"Gee, stop baby! You know I got to be on bedrest. Plus, I'm so tired."

Gee wasn't trying to hear that. I was still woozy from the medicine so all I could do was lay there.

"You got back quick," I said still halfway asleep. Gee didn't respond to me.

I started to doze back off. Gee continued to rub on my body and then kissed on my thigh. The next thing I knew, Gee was eating this pussy like he missed his meal for today. I twirled my thighs around and moved up and down on his face. The way Gee was eating my pussy had me thirsting for more. I was so worn out I could barely move, but I managed to fuck his face anyway.

"Uh uh," I moaned out loudly. My pussy was so wet I could hear every drip. I reached my hand out to put it on Gee's head to push his face closer in my pussy, and then I realized the person that what eating me out like a porn star had braids. Gee doesn't have braids.

"What the fuck! Who the fuck are you?"

"Bitch, your worst nightmare."

I started screaming as loud as I could, "Help! Help me please!"

"Bitch, shut up before I put a hot one in your ass."

"Do you know who you fucking with, bitch ass nigga," I said, with my words slurring.

"I really don't give a fuck. Now get the fuck up."

He clenched me by my hair and threw me over his shoulder. I tried to kick and punch, but I had no energy. I felt like I was being punished for everything I did to Gee. I cried out loud as he carried me down the stairs. When we made it downstairs, Gee was coming in.

"Who the fuck is you? Put my girl down before I blow your fucking head off," Gee yelled, drawing his gun out, walking towards this unknown man.

"Nigga, yo' bitch head going to get blown off first," the man said, throwing me off his shoulder, putting his forearm around my neck, and putting his pistol to my temple.

"Please don't shoot me, I'm pregnant! Please."

"Tell yo' man to put his gun down."

"Gee baby, please put the gun down. Please!"

"Fuck this nigga. I'm not doing shit. He can suck my dick, bitch ass," Gee's nostrils flared and he bit his bottom lip.

Pow! Pow!

Cage

My heart was racing fast and my hand was shaking as I pointed the gun toward Blaze. I couldn't believe what I'd just heard. This can't be true! I'm falling for my own sister. My eyes filled with tears. I wanted to kill Blaze and myself. I felt sick to the stomach.

"I don't believe you, show me some proof before I shoot you."

"This is all the proof I have right here, Derrick!"

"How the fuck you know my real name?"

"It said it right here on this note." Blaze started walking towards me.

"Don't come any closer or I swear you gon' die hoe! Sit the paper and pictures on the table."

Blaze sat everything down, held her hands up and backed away from the table. I snatched everything off the table and started looking over all the details. She had pictures from when I was younger up until now. She also had a family picture of me, my father, my mom, my other sister, and her. There was no doubt in my mind Blaze was telling me the truth. I knew I had another sister but damn, why Blaze? I lowered my gun down slowly and put it back on my side.

All I could do was stare at Blaze in disbelief. I sat down on the couch, put my head down, and began to shed some tears.

Blaze came over, rubbed my back, and said, "I'm sorry. I'm so sorry."

"You don't have to apologize, it's not your fault," I sobbed. It felt like I was in a dream and I was waiting on Blaze or somebody to wake me up.

"Look, I know this hard for you, Cage, but it's hard for me also. So, do this mean it's over between us?"

"Hell yeah! You think I'm about to fuck my sister?" I looked at Blaze with a disgusted face.

"I mean, you was just eating me up like your favorite snack."

"Bitch, that's because I didn't know I was fucking my sister. You sick."

"I'm sorry Cage, it's just I have not loved a man in so long I forgot how it felt until I met you."

"Yeah, you crazy and bipolar, just like mama."

"Fuck you, Cage!"

"Naw, I'm good!" I replied sarcastically.

I didn't know what I was going to do. Gee had paid me the money to kill Blaze but I can't kill my flesh and blood. I already knew he wasn't trying to hear this shit. I got off the couch and walked to the bathroom to call Gee. I didn't know what I was about to tell him, I wanted to tell the truth, but I couldn't tell anybody I was fucking my sister. I dialed Gee but I didn't get an answer. I guess that was God telling I needed to wait before I told Gee. I splashed some water on my face and headed for the door. Blaze stopped me in my tracks.

"Where are you going?" Blaze walked over to the door, blocking it.

"Man, move your ass out the way, Blaze."

"Please don't leave, Cage. Please."

"Blaze, we have nothing to talk about."

Chaos

"Nigga, reveal yourself you walking up on us in all black," I said aiming my pistol at my target.

"Look brah, I'm not coming for y'all. I'm not trying to rob y'all or nothing."

"Well, why the fuck you walking up on us? What's the problem?" TK replied with a serious attitude.

"I'm just here to pay back my ex-bitch for some hurt she caused me."

My mind instantly started racing. If this nigga said he was here to off Blaze then we didn't have to kidnap her ass. I could tell by dude's voice and how he talked he was about his business. Whatever Blaze did to him, if it's Blaze, she was about to be in a whole world of trouble. Not only that, it's already a hit man in there. Things were definitely about to get ugly.

"Who is yo' ex bitch?" I asked, still aiming the gun towards his head.

"Blake, but word on the street the bitch changed her name to Blaze."

TK and I looked at each other with a shocked look. You would've thought we saw a ghost. I lowered my gun just a little.

"I assume you know my ex, you on her front porch."

"Awwww shit, I thought this was a hoe I used to fuck with a long time ago house," I said, lying to this unknown person's face.

"Yeah, whatever. I don't care what y'all here for, I'm just trying to complete my mission and be on my way," the anonymous man said.

"Aight. Handle your business, my man," I said and told TK to come on.

"Yeah I am. When she sees Jason on her doorstep, she gon' shit on herself. Matter of fact I'mma surprise her when she don't have company. I think I'll come back tomorrow," Jason said. Me and TK continued walking to the car.

"That nigga about to take Blaze ass out," TK alleged while we sat in the car rolling up another Kush joint. My phone began to ring. It was Gee calling.

"What up fam?"

"Get here ASAP! Don't waste no fucking time. I don't give a fuck if you have to run every motherfucking red light on the way here! Get here *fast*," Gee hung up not giving me time to respond. I told TK to put the petal to the metal *fast*. We had to get to Gee's spot ASAP.

Kandi

I wonder who car that is? I said to myself as pulled up in front of Blaze's house. I didn't see TK or Chaos around. I wondered where those niggas were really at. I sat there, watching Blaze's house, trying to decide whether I should go in and beat this bitch's ass or kill her since I'm already here. If I killed her, nobody would know. I was the only person here to witness it right now. Yeah, I think I might just kill her ass and not tell a soul, not even TK, the man I lay with every night. I had a feeling that TK was going to find out I slept with Blaze and it was going to cause a big disaster. Before I let that happen, I would kill this bitch myself. I reached under my seat and grabbed my bottle of Grey Goose and sat there as I watched Blaze's house. My cell phone started to vibrate. I looked down and it was TK.

"Where the fuck you at?" TK yelled.

"Naw, where the fuck you at is the question," I responded, sarcastically.

"Kandi, I don't got time for your smart ass mouth right now."

"But you got time to do everything else."

"Man, shut up! What the fuck is everything else, Kandi? Huh? Huh?'

"Y'all need to shut that weak ass shit up and tell her what's up!" Chaos shouted in the background.

"Tell Chaos to mind his business before I cuss his ass out too," I hollered through the receiver of my phone.

"Can you listen for just a minute, please? Damn!"

"Whatever! Go ahead, TK!"

"Gee just called Chaos saying it's an emergency and we need to get there ASAP. I don't know what the fuck going on, but it ain't good."

"Oh my God! Oh my God! Is Shannon ok?"

"I don't know, we on our way there now. So, the question still stands, where you at?"

"I'm on the Westside. I'll meet you at Gee and Shannon house in a sec."

"Westside?" TK questioned.

"Yeah, the Westside. I will explain it when I arrive to Shannon house."

TK instantly hung up without saying bye or anything. I already knew he was mad. I took a couple of sips of my Grey Goose, put my key in the ignition, and headed to Shannon's house. I didn't know what was going on, but I knew it was serious. I could tell by the way TK sounded. I didn't know what I was about to pull up to when I got to Shannon's house, but good thing I had my pistol. If anything crazy popped off I was letting loose my whole clip.

I dialed up Shannon to see if I could find out what was going on, but her phone kept going to voicemail. Shannon's phone is barely ever dead. I immediately started to panic. The more I thought about it, the faster I drove.

Gee

"Who the fuck sent you?" I questioned the mysterious guy and walked over to him as he laid on the floor with a bullet hole in his leg.

"Nigga, fuck you. I ain't telling you shit."

"Shannon baby, get that nigga gun off the floor."

I stood over the unknown man, looking down at him, pointing the gun in his face. Shannon picked the gun up off the floor and aimed it toward the man.

"Shannon sit down, I got this. Just make sure you keep that gun close to you," I said to her before turning back to the man.

"Now, I'mma ask you one more time, my man. Who the fuck sent you?"

"Your mama sent me, bitch ass nigga."

Before I knew it, I was pistol whipping this nigga. Just the thought of him touching my woman drove me crazy.

"Gee, stop, you going to kill him! Please stop."

"Shannon, fuck this nigga. He deserves to die. He didn't give a fuck about your life."

"Gee, I know, but if you kill him we won't know why he here and who sent him."

"You're right. Keep the gun aimed at him. I'm about to drag this nigga to the basement and torture this nigga until he talks."

"Bring your bitch ass on," I shouted, dragging the nigga by his collar.

"Ahh shit, brah," he yelled as I dragged his bloody body down my basement steps, making sure his head hit every last step.

"You think you hollering now, wait 'til my brothers get here, homey."

I told Shannon to hold my pistol so I could sit him in the chair. Blood ran into his eyes from the big gash I'd put in his head. I got my pistol back from Shannon and told her to take a seat. The last thing I needed right now was for Shannon to be back in the hospital. I wasn't taking my eyes off of her ever again.

"Either you tell me who sent you, or I'm going to kill you. Now I'm going to give you time to think about it before my brothers get here."

The unfamiliar man looked up at me with blood still dripping into his eyes and said, "Nigga fuck you! You going to have to kill me."

I looked him dead in his bloody ass face and said, "you must not know who you fucking with." I gave a grimy smile then patiently waited on TK and Chaos to come. As soon as I picked up my phone to see where they were, they came bursting through the door.

"Brah, where you at?" Chaos yelled.

"I'm down here in the basement," I said, standing at the bottom of the basement steps. Chaos immediately opened the door and ran down the steps with TK following right behind him.

"What's going on?" Chaos question holding his pistol in his hand.

"I'll tell you what's going on. He tried to rape me and kidnap me," Shannon shouted.

"What, hoe ass nigga? You tried to rape my sister, huh? Huh? Lift your head up, nigga. Don't hold your head down now."

The unknown guy slowly lifted his head up. You could tell he was in pain. Chaos stood there with anger in his face, waiting on the unknown man to reveal his face. When he finally did, Chaos was shock.

"Man, oh hell naw! O Dog?"

"You know this nigga," TK and I asked at the same time.

"Yeah, this my nigga. He cool peoples. He from the Bronx."

"Yeah, I can tell that nigga was from somewhere else the way his dumb ass was talking," I replied.

"Gee and TK, let me holler at y'all ASAP," Chaos requested. We all walked over to the steps to see what Chaos had to tell us.

"We got to kill this nigga. If we don't, we going to have an army of niggas after us," Chaos whispered to us.

"Shit! I got an army, too. I don't give a fuck about going to war when it come to my loved ones," Gee replied.

"But we don't need no heat on us either, Gee, so I got to agree with Chaos on this one. I'm not trying to be watching my back or going back to jail over no bullshit," TK agreed with Chaos.

"Alright, so we going to take this nigga out right," Chaos asked.

"Hell yeah," I answered.

"Shannon baby, go make sure the house is locked up and turn on some music. Don't come back down here."

Shannon said okay and went to go secure the house.

Chaos walked over to O Dog and asked him, "Who sent you? This my sister and you tried to rape her. You know that's automatic death sentence. Just answer the question and you'll be free to go."

You could tell O Dog was in pain. He could barely hold his head up and he was losing a lot of blood. You could see the pain in his face.

Barely gaining the strength to lift up his head, he stared Chaos in his eyes.

"Blaze sent me, but I swear I didn't know this was your sister. I wouldn't disrespect like that, Chaos. I know how you get down," O Dog responded in a raspy, shaky voice.

"Oh yeah? Blaze sent you for my sister? Okay that's why her ass going to die just like your ass!"

Pow! Pow! Pow! Pow!

Chaos lit O Dog's ass up like some fire crackers on the Fourth of July.

"Go get a blanket, some cleaning supplies, and let's get rid of this body."

Cage

"Why you blocking the door, Blaze? We don't have shit to talk about. unless it's some sister and brother type shit, I don't even feel right talking to you period," I said, trying to leave. "I should have killed your ass like Gee told me when I had the chance," I mumbled under my breath.

"What you just say, Cage?"

"Nothing, man. Nothing."

"Gee sent you to kill me?"

"That's not what I said, Blaze."

"What the fuck did you say, then?"

"Move out my way so I can go, Blaze."

"I'm not moving nowhere until you answer me."

"Yeah, he sent me! You happy now? And I wish I would've took your ass out, too."

"So, you telling me you weren't feeling this shit at all? It was all a lie just to kill me?"

"Yeah, I was until I found out you was my fucking sister! That's some sick ass shit! I just fucked my sister, Blaze, and not to mention I nutted in you."

"Cage, just take a seat. I got to talk to you about one more thing."

"What part you don't understand? I don't want to talk to your ass at all. I'm cool on you for now. I just need to go home and relax my mind for a while. Can I do that? You blocking the door like you holding me hostage and shit."

"Can you please sit down just for a second? This won't take long at all, I promise you that."

"You lucky I don't hit females, or I would've slappeds the shit out your ass," I said and walked back to take a seat on the couch.

"I mean, you won't hit a female, but you will kill one!? You got your priorities fucked up," Blaze said sarcastically.

"Look who talking about priorities! Get to talking, so I can go."

"Okay, give me a second. I got to go to the restroom."

Blaze

Who the fuck this nigga think I am? I said as I stared in the mirror at myself. He was going to fuck me and kill me. He won't get away this shit at all.

I came out of the bathroom and went into my room to get my gun from under my pillow. Cage had the right one. Brother or not, I was about to kill his ass. That'll show him not to play with me. I started walking back into the living room with my gun behind my back.

"Now, what I wanted to talk to you about…" I looked up only to see Cage gone.

"Fuck!" I shouted loudly. I ran and grabbed my cell phone off the kitchen table, sat my gun down, and start calling Cage but I got no answer.

I locked my door and began walking to my room. I was so mad I had flames lit up inside of me. Before I could even make it to my room, there was a big ass boom boom at my door. Oh now this nigga want to come back, I said to myself as I snatched my pistol off the table.

"Why you leave," I said as I swung the door open with one hand, the other hand holding my pistol.

I lost my breath when I swung that door open. I couldn't believe my eyes.

"Oh my God, Jason! What are you doing here?"

"You don't look happy to see me, baby! You miss me?"

"Yeah, of course, I miss you."

He smiled at me and said, "Lie to my face again, I will beat your ass right here."

Jason slammed the door and started walking up on me. I had my gun behind my back trying to cock it, but I couldn't. Jason grabbed me by my throat and started choking the life from me. My gun instantly dropped out of my hand. He held me off the ground with my feet dangling and then threw me on the floor. I was terrified because I knew what Jason was capable of and I knew he would kill me.

"So you been here in ATL giving all my goods away? You left me to be a hoe?"

"No, I left you because you were crazy as fuck."

"You made me crazy Blake," Jason said as he climbed on top of me.

I started thinking of a plan immediately because I knew Jason is going to take my life and there were no ifs, ands, whats, or buts about that. I didn't know if what I was about to do was going to work, but it was worth a try. While Jason sat on top me, I gripped his shirt and pulled him closer to me. I began to kiss him, sticking my tongue all in his mouth. Immediately, Jason started getting in the mood. I can't lie my pussy started dripping, too.

"Damn, girl, I missed you."

"I missed you too, baby."

"If you miss me why did you leave then, huh?" Jason asked, looking at me with rage in his eyes. I had to take his mind back off of that before he flipped out and killed me because this nigga's temper was horrible.

"I'm sorry. I promise I was scared you was going to kill me. Let me make it up to you, please."

I could tell he was kind of convinced. I continued to kiss him. Jason pulled off my robe, panties, and bra. I had him ready. He got off of me, stood up and reached for my hand, pulling me off the floor.

"You still sexy. Why don't you get down and give me some boss head."

I got down on my knees and sucked the shit out his dick. I'm talking sloppy head. The kind of head that had a nigga's toes curling. I was actually missing this dick the more I sucked it.

"AWWW! That head the fucking best Blake," he moaned as he motioned my head back and forth. He was loving every moment of it.

"Bend that ass over doggy style," he commanded. I got down on all fours. I made sure I had I deep arch in my back so Jason could see how fat my ass had gotten and how it spread out.

"Oh my God! I'm about to beat this pussy up something nasty."

Jason got behind me. I was expecting his dick to go in my pussy. Instead, his face went into my ass. He started eating my ass like it was groceries, but this wasn't anything new to me. Jason was always a nasty ass nigga when it came to me, and I loved it. He spit in my ass and rubbed his tongue up and down my ass crack. That shit felt so good. After that, he started literally sucking my ass hole and sticking his tongue deep in it. I made my ass clap on his face as I looked back at it. He then stuck his fat, nine-inch dick inside of me. His dick wasn't really long, but it was fat as fuck, and it would do damage. He gripped me by my hips and started shoving all his dick in me. He gripped my hair with one hand, and the other hand gripped my hip.

"I missed this fucking pussy," he groaned as he hit that shit really fast, not stopping.

"Oh God, I can't take it! I can't take it!"

"You gone take this dick! All of it, you hear me?"

"Yes, I hear you. I'mma take that dick, baby."

Jason was the only nigga that ever made me tap out like that. I kept trying to get away from the dick. Every time I tried to run he hit it harder and gripped my hair and hips tighter. He finally stopped and told me to get on top. I started riding him backward so he could see how I made this ass shake. I could tell he was aroused because his dick was hard as fuck and he was moaning before I could even begin riding him. I bounced up and down on his dick. Each time I came down, I made my ass cheeks jump one at a time. It was driving him crazy. Jason slapped me on my ass so hard it was stinging, but I loved that shit. I got off his dick and stood over his face, then dropped down and did a split on his face. I rode the shit out of his face and came so many times that when I got up, my juices were all over his face and running down his neck.

He be eating the fuck out my pussy. I sure do miss this shit, I said to myself.

"Let me hit that ass one more time from the back."

I got in position, and Jason started beating this pussy, gripping my hips so tight he was digging his nails into them. He was deep stroking that pussy.

"Spread them ass cheeks," he demanded.

I spread my ass cheeks wide open, and he began to fuck me harder and harder. Next thing you know, he nutted all in my ass crack. I could feel it dripping from my crack to my pussy.

"Ahhhhhhh shit! Ahh shit, that pussy was just good as fuck," he said.

"I know," I replied and gave him a smile. Now I had to kill this nigga. I just had to convince him to stay so he could fall asleep, then I would just shoot him in his sleep.

"Hey, want to stay tonight? I miss you, baby."

Jason chuckled. "Stay?" he repeated. "I don't think that's a good idea, Blake. Plus, I got some shit to take care of in the morning."

Fuck now what I'm going to do, I thought.

"Okay, well can I see you tomorrow?"

"Of course," Jason gave me a smile as he got dressed.

"Okay."

Jason continued to get dressed and gave me hug, then left.

Jason

This bitch must think I'm crazy to sit up here and think I'm about to fall asleep in her bed. She had lost her fucking mind. I knew how that bitch was when she off her medicine. I would never be a fool like that, but tomorrow it's on. I'm killing her dumb ass point blank. I should have done it tonight, but she was looking so sexy I had to fuck her ass one time. Why not get that pussy one last time? She won't have any use for it anymore anyway. I had to fuck Blake without feelings because I knew if I didn't I would've fallen into her trap. With knowing how that crazy girl was, I wasn't doing that at all.

I headed to the hotel I was staying in because I was tired from fucking the shit out of Blaze. When I arrived at my hotel, I went in and took a shower. I couldn't wait to see Blaze tomorrow because that ass was as good as dead, and that's on my mama.

Kandi

I arrived at Shannon's house with my heart pounding because I knew something wasn't right. I ran up to the door and turned the knob, but it was locked. I knocked on the door, and Shannon opened it.

"What's going on, Shannon? I got here quick as I could."

I could tell Shannon had been crying from the dried up tears on her cheeks.

"He tried to rape me and kidnap me," Shannon began to cry.

"Who tried to rape and kidnap you? Huh?"

"I don't know, somebody Blaze hired."

"Blaze? Oh hell naw!"

"And… and," Shannon stuttered.

"And what?"

"Chaos killed him."

"Oh my God. Where is they at now?"

"Downstairs in the basement."

I ran downstairs to see what was going on. There was blood everywhere, but they were cleaning it up. The man they shot was wrapped in a blanket, but his feet were hanging out.

"Kandi baby, come here," TK said, giving me a hug. "Go upstairs, you don't need to see this shit."

"Okay," I went back upstairs with Shannon.

I was so scared. I understood why they killed him, but I was nervous for TK. I couldn't afford to lose my man to the system again. I loved him so much I didn't know what I would do without him. But I know one thing, Blaze got it coming.

Gee

"Let's get this nigga up out of here," I told Chaos and TK.

We picked the body up and headed upstairs. When we made it outside, Gee popped the trunk, and we threw the body in there.

"I got an idea! Let's set Blaze up like she killed this nigga," I suggested as we stood outside my luxury ride.

"How we gon' do that?" TK asked.

"We going to watch that bitch house and when she leaves, we going to put the body in there and get all the prints off."

"Hell naw, the prints might not be all the way off, and then that shit can lead back to me," Chaos explained.

"You right, let's just leave the body there at her house then have Shannon or Kandi call the police on her ass."

"Naw, I got a better idea," Chaos proclaimed."

"We got to think of something ASAP because this body going to start stanking and I can't have that smell in my ride."

"Okay, this what we going to do tomorrow night, I'mma go to Blaze house and ask her have she seen Shannon because she been missing for a couple days. Blaze going to think that Shannon been kidnap by O Dog and her mission is done. I'm going to get Blaze to help me go look for her. Of course, she's going to go, and when I text and give you the word, just be ready to drop the body in there and have Shannon or Kandi to call the police," Chaos said, hitting his black and mild with an evil grin on his face.

"Hell yeah, I love that plan," TK and I both agreed.

"Hold on, did that nigga have a cell phone on him?" TK asked

"That's a good fucking question. Pop the trunk and check his pocket, Gee," Chaos said.

"Nigga, hell naw! I'm not touching his dead ass,"

"Nigga, move your bitch ass out the way and pop the trunk. You act like this the living dead and shit," Chaos said.

TK and I burst out laughing.

I popped the trunk and Chaos went in his pocket and found a cell phone and a couple of bands. Chaos turned off his location so the phone company couldn't track him. As soon as he did that, Blaze texted and asked was the mission complete. Chaos texted back, acting like O Dog, letting her know that everything was good. She responded with a smiley face emoji and said, "See you tomorrow night about seven-thirty."

This is about to be an easy ass job, I thought to myself. We all departed and agreed to meet up tomorrow.

Cage

As bad as I didn't want to call Gee and tell him what's going on, I had to, it's only right. We go way back, and I hoped he'd understand where I'm coming from when I let him know I couldn't kill Blaze and the reason why. I reached in my pocket, got my cell phone out, and began to call Gee. I didn't know whether he was going to answer or not. I'd called a couple of times he hadn't answered or called back.

"Yeah," Gee answered.

"What up, brah. I need to talk to you in person ASAP."

"Whatever you got to say me can be said over the phone, my nigga."

"Damn, why you getting so defensive, my nigga." I assumed Gee must have known something or heard something the way he was coming at me.

"What you got to say? I'm busy," Gee replied sarcastically.

"Look, Blaze is not dead. I can't kill her."

"What! What the fuck you mean you can't kill her?"

"Man look, I started fucking her trying to reel her in and just get close to her so I can make my job easier right…"

"You were fucking that bitch?" Gee questioned, cutting me off.

"Look, let me tell you. Yeah, I fucked her a couple of times, but only to get close to her, that's it. Then, one day we was chilling, and I was about to kill her, and she drops this envelope with pictures of me and my family. I pulled my gun on her and asked where she got the pictures from. Then the bitch tells me she's my sister and shows me proof."

"Man, what the fuck!"

"Yeah, so I start feeling bad like damn I can't kill my sister. Even though I don't know her like that brah, my heart wouldn't let me do it."

"I feel you, brah. That's some hard shit to swallow right there. But I got one question."

"What's that, Gee?"

"When can I get my money back?"

"I got it for you right now."

"Alright, meet down at the hiking park in about a half an hour with it."

"Alright, I got you."

Me and Gee hung up. That conversation didn't go as bad as I thought, but I wasn't feeling how Gee was coming at me. But I had to understand, because if it was my money I would be pissed, too.

Gee

Tonight was not my night. We already bodied a nigga, and here Cage goes calling me with this bogus ass story. Why won't he just admit to it he fucked that bitch and fell for her? Even if he is telling the truth, he didn't know Blaze was his sister at the time he was fucking her, so that's no excuse. If he would've just got in and out the pussy and done his job that would've been a different scenario. I slipped on some clothes, grabbed Shannon's car keys, and told her I would be right back. Kandi was still there with her. When I arrived at the park, Cage wasn't there yet. I waited around for like twenty minutes and he finally pulled up. Cage hopped out the car looking fly, with the money inside of the duffle bag.

"My bad again. I hope you understand I'm not on no bullshit," Cage proclaimed as he handed me the duffle bag.

I opened it up to see if all the money was in there. When I saw it was, I threw it through the passenger side window.

"Alright, no hard feelings," I said, with my hand in my pocket, gripping my pistol with the silencer on it. I couldn't trust Cage's ass, so he had to die.

Cage started walking to his car after we shook hands.

"Ahy Cage," I said aggressively.

"Yeah," Cage answered with one foot in the car and the other one out.

Pow! Pow! Pow! Pow!

I lit his bitch ass up. He thought he was about to get away with the shit he did, he could think again.

Cage's body fell to the ground, and I dragged him to the back of the car. I tried to get his body in the trunk, but I couldn't. I struggled for about ten minutes, and I finally got his ass in the trunk praying that nobody saw me. I snatched his keys off the ground, got out the car, and sped off.

I got home and started feeling crazy. It seemed like my life was falling apart even more. I had two dead bodies on my property, and if shit didn't go right, I could end up in jail for a long time. But right now I had to explain to TK and Chaos why I had another fucking body. The whole night I couldn't sleep. I tossed and turned and before I knew it, morning had arrived. I got up and got myself together. This was going to be a long day, I could feel it. It seemed like time was going so slowly. About a quarter 'til five Chaos and TK arrived at my house.

Chaos

"Y'all ready to do this shit," I asked, with a serious face.

"Hell yeah," Gee yelled, hyped up.

"But we got a problem, man."

"What's that?" I probed with a confused face.

"I killed Cage last night and he in Shannon's trunk."

"What the fuck?" me and TK shouted at the same time.

"Man, I had to. This nigga called me with some bullshit ass story that Blaze was his sister, and he was fucking her. But he didn't know she was his sister until after he fucked her. I felt like this nigga wasn't loyal and he might tell Blaze I sent him. So, I took his ass out."

"Man, that's some foul ass shit. But damn I wish you would had hollered at us first, Gee," I shook my head getting pissed off.

"Wait. Hold on y'all, think about it," TK shouted out.

"Think about what?" We ask looking dumbfounded.

"If Blaze and Cage was fucking and we put O Dog in the house too, that's going to be the perfect murder. It's going to look like O Dog and Cage got into it over Blaze, they all was fighting, and then they both end up dead. And because Blaze is still alive, the police going want to know how did that happen. And of course Blaze not going to know what to say. Damn, I'm good."

"Hell the fuck yeah," I screamed out loud. "Let's do this shit."

We went outside and threw Cage's body in the trunk with O Dog.

"Look TK, you ride with Gee. When me and Blaze on the way back from acting like we looking for Shannon, I'm going to give you the okay to call Shannon and Kandi. Make sure y'all explain everything they should do."

They both agreed. I headed to Blaze's house, and they left fifteen minutes after me. I arrived at Blaze's house about a half hour later. I was nervous as hell to knock on this hoe's door because I didn't know if she was going to fall for the bullshit I was feeding her.

Knock Knock

"Who is it?"

"Chaos."

"Who?"

"Chaos. Shannon's brother."

She got quiet and then the door finally opened. I could tell she was shook.

"What up, Blaze. I need you help ASAP."

"What's wrong," Blaze asked, looking confused but I could tell deep down she was nervous as fuck.

"Look, I know this might sound crazy, but Shannon is missing, and I need your help finding her."

"Oh my God, what! Oh my God, no," Blaze's fake as yelled as if she was so hurt Shannon was missing. "Hold on let me slip on my Air Force Ones. Come in."

Blaze walked to her room, and I noticed a gun sitting on her table. This was about to be good because the gun that was sitting on the table was the same kind of gun I shot O Dog with.

"Okay, I'm ready," Blaze announced as she walked out of the room with some tight fitted jeans, that hugged her thick thighs and fat ass, and plain white tee.

"This bitch looks good in anything she wears. Damn," I mumbled to myself.

Blaze locked up her house. I texted Gee to let him know we were leaving out.

"So, where we going?"

"Areas by where my sister live, at parks, and shit."

Blaze caught me off-guard with that question, but it was easy to convince her to believe anything since she thought O Dog had Shannon.

Out of nowhere, Blaze started rubbing on my dick.

"Is you crazy, yo? Why you trying to rub on me at a time like this? My fucking sister missing!"

"You just so sexy. I want you."

Blaze start grabbing my dick out my pants, struggling to pull it out because of the length. My dick was hard as a rock so fuck it. Just like any nigga, I wasn't turning down any head. Blaze started playing with the head of my dick with her tongue, teasing my shit. This hoe was nasty, but her nasty ass could suck some good dick. She began slobbering on my dick, making sure every inch was in her throat. The slurping noise from my dick being so wet turned me on, but one thing about me can't no hoe turn me out, so I'm cool. She gripped my dick with both hands and began to jack it slowly.

"Ahh fuck! Suck that dick," I whispered, biting my lip. Damn, this bitch had some bomb ass head.

I made to the destination and parked. I leaned my seat back so Blaze could continue to suck the life out my dick. She started unbuttoning her pants with one of her hands and was playing with her pussy. I can hear her shit gushing as she played with it. I didn't know what she's thinking, but I wasn't about to fuck her ol' nasty ass.

She started sliding her pants down, still sucking my dick at the same time. I grabbed the back of her head and start pushing her head down on my dick. I hurried up and nutted all in that bitch's throat so she wouldn't think she was about to get fucked. You could tell she was upset that I'd nutted. She pulled her pants up, mad as hell. I was cracking up on the inside.

"You good over there?"

"Yeah I'm good. Why you ask that?"

"You look mad, that's all."

"Naw, I'm good. You good?"

"Yeah Blaze, I'm good."

Blaze was pissed to the max that she didn't get any of this monster dick. We got out the car and began to search the park. We walked around for a while, and I texted and gave Gee the okay to take the bodies in.

"How long has Shannon been missing?"

"Since yesterday."

"Why didn't no one go to the police?"

"Gee on his way there now."

"Oh," Blaze rolled her eyes. She was mad when I mentioned Gee's name.

"Well shit, it don't look like she here either. It's getting kind of dark, we can search some more places tomorrow. You took up all the time sucking my dick. Ha-ha, 'I laughed out loud.

"Fuck you," Blaze stormed off and walked to the car with an attitude.

I texted Gee to let him know to have the girls to get ready to call the police in about twenty minutes because we were on the way back to Blaze's house. Even though I was close to Blaze's house, I wanted to make sure I wasn't there when the police pulled up. When I pulled up to Blaze's house, I saw the coast was clear. She got out and began walking towards her house.

"Ahy."

"What?" Blaze turned around and looked at me with a fake ass attitude.

"Thanks for your help Blaze."

"Yeah, whatever."

I pulled off and called Gee's cell phone to see where they were.

"Where y'all niggas at?" I asked when Gee picked up the phone.

"Almost to the house."

"Man, that bitch sucked my dick and got mad because I didn't fuck her nasty ass."

"Fuck her! Shit she gon' have a variety of pussy to fuck when her ass goes to jail," Gee chuckled.

"Ha-ha! You crazy, brah."

"Where did y'all put everything at?" I said speaking in codes.

"In her room. Hopefully, she doesn't go straight in there."

"True. I will see y'all when I get there, Gee."

"Aight."

Blaze

The nerve of Chaos acting like he didn't want this pussy. He knew damn well he wanted this pussy. I poured up a drink and rolled up a joint. I reached for my cell phone on the kitchen counter so I could hit up O Dog. I couldn't wait to see Shannon's reaction when she saw me. Before I could even dial the number, there was a knock at my door. I walked to the door quietly and looked out the peephole. It was Jason.

Shit, what his ass want? I asked myself as I quietly walked away from the door. The knocking finally stopped.

Thank God he's gone, I thought as I called O Dog's phone to let him know I was on the way as soon as I took a shower. But I didn't get an answer. I began undressing as I walked to the bathroom.

"Damn I forgot my dry off towel," I said aloud to myself. I walked out of the bathroom into my bedroom and almost fainted.

"Oh my God! Oh my God! Cage! O Dog! You okay? Get up, please," I screamed and cried as I held Cage in my arms.

I noticed my gun was lying next to Cage. I grabbed it, ran to the bathroom sink, and started washing the blood off of me from Cage. I quickly ran out of the bathroom, grabbed the clothes I had on off the floor, and put them on. Then there was a knock at the door. I knew it was Jason and I needed him to get rid of these bodies and help me. I ran to open the door and, to my surprise, it was the police.

"Get down on the floor now! Get down," the officer yelled loudly and aggressively.

"I didn't do shit," I yelled as I got down on the floor. When I saw the other officers walk back to the room, I already knew my life was over. I was going to jail for life.

One officer handcuffed me and walked me out to the police car. When he shut that door, I knew I wasn't getting out of this shit.

"Officer, please listen to me. I didn't do this! Somebody setting me up."

The officer laughed, "And I'm boo boo the fool. That's what they all say. Tell it to the judge."

The officer chuckled and walked away, leaving me in the back seat while he went back into my place. Tears began to run down my face. I looked over to the left and saw Jason sitting in his car shaking his head. Then he drove off. All I could think about was who set me the fuck up. I had I good idea, though. I think it was Shannon. She must have gotten away from O Dog and had Gee kill him. But, there was no way she could've escaped O Dog.

Chaos

As soon as I walked through the door at Gee's house, they started popping champagne bottles and pouring drinks.

I laughed out loud at the fact they were celebrating Blaze going to jail, but fuck it. I joined the party. They even had the TV on, waiting on the news. *Man, I love my family*, I thought to myself.

"Gee, TK, Shannon, and Kandi, I love y'all. But I'm going to say this one time only, what we did better not go out this circle or we all going to jail. We got to take this to our graves."

Everybody agreed on it, and we all sat around drinking, waiting for the news to come on. But before the news got a chance to come on, the screen flashed saying, "Breaking news: two men have been found dead on the Westside. Police have a suspect in custody by the name of Blake Johnson. Police believe this was a love triangle gone wrong. Stay tuned for further updates." We all started cheering and jumping around happy as hell that everything worked out for the best.

"I will like to make a toast," Gee said.

We all held our cups up, except for Shannon pregnant ass.

"I just wanted to say I love all of you and I'm happy this crazy bitch going to jail. So let's toast to a happy life, and my soon-to-be wife," Gee smiled and kissed Shannon and her stomach.

We all toasted to a happy life and his soon-to-be wife and then we took our drinks to the head.

Blaze

When I heard those bars shut, I instantly started screaming and crying. I went crazy. I started punching the wall, biting myself, and scratching myself. I couldn't handle it. The officers ran in and started restraining me. I couldn't believe I was sitting behind bars. They took me to the psych ward, strapped me down, and gave me a shot. The whole time I was strapped down all I could think about was revenge is mine. *I don't know how Shannon did it, but what I do know is her and Gee got it coming,* I said to myself with an evil smile on my face.

Shannon

One year later

It's a year later, and me and Gee finally tied the knot, not to mention we have a beautiful baby girl who is eight months old now. After all the shit me and Gee went through, we deserved to get married. I hate what I took him through, and I promise him I will never hurt him again. Life has been so wonderful between Gee and I. We don't get to go out and have fun like we used to because Gee doesn't trust anybody with our child unless it's family, and hell, he barely trusted them. I've been searching for another job, but Gee doesn't want me to work. He keeps telling me to come work for him and do his accounting. I've been thinking about it, but I'm not sure. My doorbell rang, disturbing my thoughts.

"Who is it?"

"Me. Open the door," Kandi said.

I opened the door and invited Kandi in.

"Here, I checked your mailbox. Don't say I never did nothing for you." Kandi laughed and handed me my mail.

I went through my mail, and it was nothing but a bunch of damn bills.

"You could've left this in there," I stated, throwing the mail on the table in front of Kandi.

We looked at each other and laughed.

"Girl, you didn't even go through all the mail," Kandi explained as she looked through the mail.

"I don't have to. I know what bills I need to pay."

"Yeah, whatever, and who writing you from an institute?" Kandi questioned.

"Nobody that I know of. Let me see that." I snatched the envelope out of Kandi's hand and opened it.

I didn't even bother to read the front of the envelope, I just tore it open. I pulled the letter out and read it.

Dear Shannon,

First I want to apologize and tell you I'm sorry for all the hurt and pain I caused you. I never meant to hurt you or cause you any harm. I know you are probably reading this letter with your pretty face frown up. I just want you to find it in your heart to forgive me. I been locked up all this time, and all I can do is think about you. I hope you're happy and I wish you nothing but the best.

Love always, Blaze.

I ripped the letter up and threw it in the trash.

"What's wrong with you?" Kandi looked at me with a confused expression on her face.

"That was a letter from Blaze's crazy ass."

"What! What did she say?"

"Girl, nothing. Just talking about she apologizes for everything she's done to me."

"Fuck that bitch. She lucky her ass locked up in that nut house, or I would beat her motherfucking ass."

"You and me both," I replied.

There was a knock on the door.

"That must be Kia," I said as I walked to the door.

"I don't like that bitch. It' something about her," Kandi said as she followed me.

"Kandi, please chill out. Kia is cool, plus it ain't like we friends. We just work out together."

"Yeah, whatever. I still don't like her ass." Kandi rolled her eyes.

"Hey, Kia, come in. I just got to grab my keys and my gym bag. I will down in a minute."

"Okay, cool."

Kia came in, and I could see Kandi mugging her out the corner of my eye.

"Problem?" Kia asked, looking Kandi up and down.

"Hell yeah, bitch it's a problem, hoe! Fuck you mean!" Kandi got in Kia's face and stared her dead in her eyes.

"Ahy, cut that shit out in my house," I stated, interrupting Kandi and Kia's petty argument.

"I don't like her ass," Kandi said and walked over to the couch and sat down.

"Kandi, there are bottles in the refrigerator for Gia. Call me if you need me."

"Umm hmm," Kandi replied with a funky attitude.

For some reason, Kandi did not like Kia. She didn't know her from a can of paint, but every time I asked Kandi what was her problem with Kia, she would say 'I just don't like her ass it's something about her. She got this sneaky ass demeanor to her.' I think Kandi was just jealous that I was cool with Kia. Kia never disrespected Kandi or said anything offensive to her, but every time she sees Kia, she looked at her sideways or said something smart. I don't blame Kia for asking Kandi if she has a problem.

Kandi

I don't know why Shannon be taking up for that bitch Kia. Anybody can look at her and tell she a snake in the damn grass. The way she carries herself is slutty, and she got a stank attitude like she the shit. I mean, don't get me wrong, she ain't ugly, but she isn't all that either. I guess u can say she's average. Me personally, I don't trust no bitch I don't know. They all sneaky to me, but you can't tell Shannon shit with her friendly ass. That's why her ass got caught up with Blaze, she was too damn friendly. Even though she and Kia are just gym partners, I get a bad vibe from her. I see how she looks around Shannon's house like she wishes this was her house. If I find out that she crossed the line with Shannon, I'm whooping her ass on site.

Anyway, TK been acting kind of weird lately. I don't know what has gotten into his ass. He called and told me he needed to talk to me ASAP, and it was urgent. When he told me that, all types of thoughts started to cross my mind. I know one thing, if TK tells me he's cheating on me or he got a bitch pregnant, I'm whooping her ass and his. TK walked into Shannon's house throwing my thoughts off. Soon as he came in, he slammed the door and joined me on the couch.

I instantly attacked him with my words when he sat down. "So, what the fuck you got to tell me? You better not be fucking around." I rolled my neck and eyes.

"First off, chill the fuck out! I'm not fucking with no bitch, but I heard you was! So, what up with that."

"What! What bitch?" I acted stupid like I didn't know what TK was talking about.

I knew he was talking about Blaze, but I was trying to borrow time to think of a lie. If TK found out I slept with Blaze, ain't no telling what he might do, and I don't feel like arguing with him.

"You didn't mess around with no woman while I was in jail?

"Who told you that?"

"Don't worry about who the fuck told me, Kandi," TK said in an angry tone, pointing his finger in my face.

"I don't know what you talking about." I played stupid, knowing damn well I knew.

"Oh, so now you lying to me?" TK pulled out his phone and started dialing a number.

"Who you calling?" My heart began to race.

"You will see."

I snatched the phone out of TK's hand and hung it up.

"Why the fuck you hang up?" TK shouted.

Tears started to form in my eyes, and all I could do was drop my head.

"What's wrong with you? Huh?"

"I'm sorry."

"What you sorry for? You didn't do shit, remember?"

"I slept with her."

"With who?"

"Blaze," I stated.

"You couldn't be woman enough to tell me that? So, that's what you like now? Pussy."

"Hell naw, it just happened."

"It just happened, huh? Yeah, okay." TK got up and started walking to the door.

I ran behind him and grabbed his arm.

"Don't touch me, Kandi, you a fucking liar!"

"I'm sorry, can we just talk about it at least?"

"No, I will see you when you get home if I be there." TK snatched his arm away from me and left out the door.

I wanted to chase him, but I couldn't because the baby was upstairs asleep. I felt so bad for not telling TK that I slept with Blaze. When he asked me had I slept with anybody while he was locked up, I started to tell him the truth then. The only reason I didn't tell him the truth was that I thought we were going to fight about it.

TK

Damn, I can't believe Kandi fucked around on me with that bitch, Blaze. I guess Chaos was telling the truth. It's not like I didn't believe him, but I'm the type nigga who likes to find out for myself because it's too many haters out here. Not saying Chaos is a hater, but you never know. I can't believe I lasted this long without confronting her. At first, I tried to put it out of my mind. I told myself it didn't matter and to let the past be the past. But as time went on, it continued to bother me until I couldn't take it anymore. I had to confront it once and for all.

Now I feel like I can't even trust Kandi. I asked her did she sleep with anybody behind my back when I was locked up, and she told me no. If she would've told me when I asked, I wouldn't be mad at her ass. I feel like the woman lay with every night can't be trusted. I love Kandi, and I don't want it to be over between us at all, but she got me in my feelings. She got me wondering if my dick even satisfies her. I mean, she acts like it does by the way she be moaning and carrying on.

After I left Kandi, I was headed to the house, and I got a call from Gee asking if I wanted to meet up with him at the gym. I told him I would since I was already dressed for the gym. I had on a white tee and some black jogging pants. I pulled up to the gym about twenty minutes later, and Gee's car was parked outside. I parked my car in the spot next to him and headed into the gym. I showed the lady at the front desk my membership and walked to the men's locker room. I forgot I had a pair of shorts in my locker. I went to my locked and grabbed my shorts. After changing into my shorts, I removed my wallet out my jogging pants and put it in my shorts then placed my jogging pants in the locker. I never leave my wallet in the locker. I don't trust nobody. Remembering that my gym membership was due, I walked back to the front desk.

"I would like to pay my membership. It's due tomorrow." I handed the lady my credit card and identification. I'm quite sure she knows my name, as much as I come in here.

"Here you go, Mr. Kenny," the lady said, handing me my card back and a receipt.

"Thank you."

I walked away and put my credit card in my wallet. I was about to throw the receipt away until I noticed some writing on the receipt. I looked at it and saw that the lady at the front desk had slid me her number. I turned around, and she waved at me and smiled. I gave her a lil fake smile back and kept it moving. My plan was to throw the receipt away when she wasn't looking, but she had her eye on me the whole time.

"What up, nigga? I see you made it. About damn time," Gee said as I approached the bench where he was lifting weights.

"Nigga, I told your ass I was coming. It only took me twenty minutes."

"It seems like an hour, nigga."

"Naw, your ass just tired from lifting all them damn weights."

We both chuckled.

I slid the receipt I was holding into my pocket then sat on the bench next to Gee and started lifting my weights.

"So, how shit been with you and Shannon?"

"Good, but sometimes I think she be getting the urge to be with another woman."

"Damn, that's messed up for real."

"Yeah, it is, but I just keep it cool because we married now and I trust her. But, sometimes I have my doubts," Gee replied as he put the weights back and sat up on the edge of the bench.

I could tell Gee was in deep thought by the way he dropped his head down and began to shake it. I know exactly what Gee was feeling when it came to him thinking Shannon wanted another woman.

"I will be back. Let me go grab a Gatorade out the car."

Shannon

After working out for half an hour, I was drained. I usually work out for an hour or more, but the baby had kept me up all night, and I didn't get any rest at all. I went into the gym locker room and grabbed my keys and cell phone out the locker. I walked over to Kia to let her know I was about to leave. She told me that she would walk me outside. On the way out the door, Kia stopped and talked to the girl Kim at the front desk for about fifteen minutes. They are real close. I don't know what they were talking about, but I was tired as hell and ready to go. I walked out the door, leaving Kia because I was at the point where I could barely hold my damn eyes open.

"Shannon, wait up," Kia said, running behind me.

"My bad, girl, I was running my mouth with my friend. She was telling me about some nigga she just gave her number to."

"Oh, you cool. I'm just tired as hell," I replied.

"Sure you can drive? You can always ride with me, and I will bring you back to get your car," Kia suggested.

"I'm good, but thanks for the offer."

Kia reached out and hugged me, and I could have sworn I felt her rub my ass.

"Hit me up later. Maybe we can go out and have a few drinks."

"Okay."

Kia was cool, and all, but me going out with her was probably not going to happen. I don't make new friends because I hate drama, and I don't have time to be trying to figure out is the next bitch real or fake.

"Shannon?" Gee's voice said.

"Hey, baby, I didn't know you were working out today."

"You know I got to stay looking good for my wifey." Gee said and kissed me on the lips.

"Baby, this is Kia, the one I told you I be working out with."

"Oh yeah, nice to finally meet you, Kia," Gee said.

"Nice to meet you too. Well, let me get back in here. Shannon, I will see you soon."

"Okay."

Gee walked me to my car and opened the door for me. I got in and rolled the window down. Gee stood outside my window and stared at me.

"What, Gee? I know that look. What's wrong?

"I got a question, and I want you to be completely honest with me."

"Okay, what is it?"

"You still attracted to women?"

"Gee, no, I learned my lesson. Even if I was, I wouldn't dare try it again."

"Okay, I take your word." Gee leaned in the window and gave me a peck on the cheek.

"I love you."

"I love you too, Shannon, baby."

I drove off and headed home.

Gee

I love Shannon, I just hope she ain't lying to me about being with another woman. When I was walking to her car, I saw her and Kia hugging, and I could've sworn I saw Kia rub Shannon's ass. It happened so quick, I couldn't tell. I went back into the gym where TK was at, and he wasn't where I left him. I continued to work out and waited for TK to come back.

"Hey," a woman's voice said from behind me.

I turned around to see who it was, and it was Kia. She was sexy. She didn't have shit on Shannon, but she had her own look. She was light skinned, short, with long black hair, a couple of freckles on her face, and she had a nice lil shape.

"What up?" I replied, looking at Kia standing there in some pink shorts, pink sports bra, and white Nikes.

"So, how long you and Shannon been together?" she asked, looking at me and biting her lip.

"Long enough. Why you ask?"

"Do you love your wife?" she asked as she walked up on me.

"Shorty, what you on?" I interrogated her, looking dead into her sexy slanted eyes.

I don't know what this girl was on, but I can't lie, she was turning me on, and my dick was getting hard.

"Nothing, I just want to know if you are happy in your marriage." She licked her lips.

"Yeah, I'm very happy. I love my wife."

She looked at me, smiled, and said, "I bet you do."

We stood there and stared at each other for a couple of seconds until TK came over, interrupting our stare.

"What going on here?" TK asked.

"Nothing, this is Shannon's work out buddy, Kia."

"Oh," TK replied and stood there looking at me and Kia crazy.

Kia smiled and walked back to the front of the gym. I don't know what Kia called herself doing, but she had my attention. I haven't had a woman flirt with me in so long, and it was turning me all the way on. Don't get me wrong, I love my wife, and I will never do anything to hurt her. I have cheated on Shannon plenty of times before back in the day, and I'm not trying to cause her any type of hurt again. Even though my heart still got a scar on it from what she did to me, I told myself I was going to let it go and move forward with our relationship.

TK

"Shorty was looking like she wanted to get fucked," I stated to Gee.

"She better take her lil thick ass on somewhere. Shannon will kill her ass," Gee replied.

I don't know who Gee think he was fooling. I saw how he and Kia were staring at each other like they were ready to fuck the shit out of each other. I can't blame him if he does. Shorty is kind of sexy.

"I'm about to get out of here, brah," Gee said.

"Alright, I'm going to work out for a little while longer. I will hit you up."

"Alright."

Me and Gee shook hands, and he left out the door. I went back over to the weights and began to lift them.

"Ummm, I would love to see you lift me like that," a sexy voice said.

I looked up, and it was the woman from the front desk. I lifted one more weight and set it down above me.

I cracked a little fake smile, and replied, "Is that right?"

I looked her up and down, checking her out from head to toe.

"You like what you see?" she asked me.

I damn sure was liking what I saw. Lil mama was sexy as hell. She was tall with caramel skin, slim all the way around. I love my women thick, but it was something about her. I ignored her question and stood up.

"I got a woman," I replied.

"What that supposed to mean?" she questioned.

"It means I'm taken and I can't be entertaining another woman," I said and started walking away.

I looked out the corner of my eyes to see if she was trailing behind me, but she wasn't. I walked into the locker room and went into the dressing area to change back into my clothes. I was going to take a shower, but I didn't do too much working out. I opened the door, and the girl from the front desk was standing right there. Soon as I opened the door, she attacked me and pushed me back into the dressing room and locked the door. She started kissing me, sticking her tongue all down my throat. She removed her lips off mine and started kissing my neck as she rubbed my muscular arms.

"Shorty, what you doing?" I asked, pushing her back.

"Don't act like you don't want this."

"Look, I'm in a relationship. I told you that."

"I won't tell if you don't," she proclaimed and dropped to her knees then pulled my boxers and jogging pants down at the same time. My dick was solid hard. She placed her wet juicy lips on the bell head of my dick and began to suck it. I leaned back against the wall as I let her please me. She moved her tongue slowly around the tip of my dick and began to suck it she had done this repeatedly.

"Aww, fuck," I moaned in a low voice.

She finally released my dick from her mouth. She pulled up her dress, pulled down her thong, and bent over in front of me. I positioned my hands on her hips and slid my long log inside her juicy wet ocean. Her body tense up a little once I entered her.

"Don't tense up now. I thought you wanted this dick," I said in an aggressive tone.

I start hitting that pussy, and she was moaning like crazy. She kept trying to move my hands off her hips, but I kept my hands planted tightly and made her take every inch. I fucked her for a good ten minutes before it was over. I pulled my clothes back up while she fixed her thong.'

"Make sure you call me. Oh, and by the way, my name is Kim," she said before she walked out the door.

I can't believe I just fucked another woman and I loved every minute of that shit. I didn't even know this girl's name, and here I am fucking her like I've known her for years. I can't lie, that pussy was juicy, and I wouldn't mind sliding in that shit again. I feel bad a little because I love Kandi to death and the last thing I want to do is hurt her, but Kandi got me feeling like she can't be trusted. If she lied to me about Blaze, how do I know she ain't lying about messing with another man? Thoughts flooded my mind as I walked out the gym to go home.

Gee

"Aww shit! That shit feels good. Keep sucking it like that."

"You like that, daddy?"

"Hell yeah, I do."

Kia was sucking the life out my body inside my car, and I was loving that shit. She had a nigga's toes curling, and I could barely take that head. I laid the driver side seat back, and Kia climbed on top of me. She took her sports bra off, and her 34 C cups sat up in my face. Her breasts were round and juicy. She began to ride my dick slowly. I took my hands and gripped her breasts and caressed them as she rode my long log. She had some bomb ass pussy, and it was dripping wet. I disconnected my hand from her breasts and placed them on her waist line. I guided her back and forth on my dick. The look on Kia's face was so attractive. My phone began to ring, interrupting my thoughts. I looked at Kia.

She said, "Answer. I won't say nothing."

I reached into my pocket and grabbed my phone. It was Shannon calling. I wasn't going to answer it, but I didn't want her to get suspicious.

"What's up, baby?"

"Nothing. Somebody want to talk to you," Shannon stated.

She put our baby on the phone, and I could hear her making all kinds of baby noises.

"Hey, Daddy baby, I miss you."

Kia looked like she was mad that I was on the phone with Shannon and my baby. My dick instantly went soft while it was in her. All I could think about was my family right now.

"Ha-ha, she's silly." Shannon giggled as she got back on the phone.

Kia climbed off the top of me and sat on the passenger side. After that, she leaned over, gripped my penis, and started sucking it. My dick got hard again. I grasped the back of her head with my right hand and held my cell phone to my ear with my left hand.

"That's my baby, but I will be there in a minute, baby. See you when I get there," I said.

"Dang! Why you rushing me off the phone?"

"Girl, ain't nobody rushing you off the phone. I'm driving, trying to focus on this road."

"Umm hmmm, nigga you always drive and talk to me. When has that ever stopped you?"

"Okay, stay on the phone then, Shannon."

Kia lifted her head up and looked at me with an attitude. I knew Shannon wasn't going to stay on the phone. That was just my way to prove to her that I wasn't rushing her off the phone.

"Naw, go ahead. I will see your ass when you get here, and you better not take all day."

"I will," I said jokingly.

"Yeah okay! We will see, nigga," Shannon said.

I chuckled and said okay then we disconnected our call.

Kia put her mouth back on my dick and sucked the shit out of it. I told her to climb back on top of me and ride it, and she did just that. After about fifteen minutes, Kia was finished doing her thing and we both nutted. We sat and talked for another ten minutes, then I left.

Blaze

Today is the day I finally get out of this damn institution, and I can't wait. If Shannon thinks I'm not coming for revenge, she got another thing coming. They set me up and killed my brother; that's not going to fly with me. Even though I didn't know Cage like that, he still was my blood, and I know Cage would've done the same thing for me. I know this may sound crazy, but I was in love with Cage despite the fact that he was my brother. That man just did something to me that sent chills through my body. I haven't had a man touch my body the way he did in years. He was the only person that took my mind off Shannon, even though I'm still in love with Shannon.

"Blake, you've been released," one of the staff members stated, calling me by my first name.

I got up from my bed, grabbed my belongings, and walked to the door.

"You have to talk to Mrs. Angie before you can leave."

"Okay," I replied.

The staff member steered me to Mrs. Angie's office. Mrs. Angie was a counselor at the facility I was locked up in. She was older than me, in her late 40's, but she looked every bit of 30. She dressed young and had a nice body on her. She stayed calling me in her office to talk to her. I could tell by the way she looked at me that she was feeling me. One day, I guess she gathered the heart to say something to me. Mrs. Angie told me how much she had a crush on me and if I let her taste me, she would help me get out early. She also said that she would get me a good lawyer, and it will be easy to get me out early since my schizophrenia can be controlled with medicine. The judge tried to give me three years in this damn place. I took Angie up on that offer and I got another court date two weeks later and the lawyer she promised me. The judge sentenced me to a year in the institute, and that was that end of that.

I walked into Mrs. Angie's office, and she came from behind her desk and locked the door.

"Hey, Angie, you wanted to see me?" I said.

"When don't I want to see you?" She spoke in a seductive voice.

I giggled and stood up.

Angie grabbed me by the back of my head and forced me to kiss her. Next, she took off my pants and spread my legs apart. She dropped down to her knees and start feasting on my pussy. I had to admit, Angie could eat some bomb ass pussy, and she kept me satisfied the whole time I was locked up. Every Thursday or Friday she would call me into her office. I even did a couple of private dances for her. I had Angie going crazy and bringing me all type of shit, food, weed, money, clothes. You name it, I had it.

Angie took her index finger and thumb and held my pussy open. She twirled her tongue around my clit and before I knew it, I was cumming everywhere. She got off her knees and lifted her dress up and sat in the chair in front of her desk. She didn't have any panties on, I got down and knelt before her. I eased my index finger into her pussy and moved it in and out until it got super wet. I kissed all around her pussy until I got it soaking and wet. She squirmed around in the chair, letting me know that it was feeling good and she was ready to get that pussy ate. I teased her pussy with my tongue and began to eat it. Before I knew it, Angie was exploding all on my face. After catching all her juices in my mouth, I got up. She was still lying there shaking from the big orgasm she let out. Angie finally got up and pulled her dress down.

"Damn, I'm going to miss you," Angie stated as she walked over to her desk, grabbed a business card, and handed it to me.

"Thank you."

"No, thank you! Make sure you keep in touch," she said.

"I will."

I left out the door and headed to my destination. The crazy part about Angie, she is married with children, and every day her husband brings her lunch. That still didn't stop her from eating me alive. She made sure she ate me every chance she got.

Kandi

I don't know how I'm going to make this up to TK, but I got to think of something. When he's mad, he can become a pain in the ass. When I pulled up, TK was pulling up as well. I made it in the house before him.

I took my shoes off at the door and hung my keys up on the key holder right by my front door. Soon, TK walked in I attacked him and started to unbutton his pants.

"Move, get off me," TK said, removing my hand from his pants.

"Damn, you never turn this head and pussy down. What's the problem?

"You!" TK took his shoes off and went upstairs to the bathroom.

I trailed behind him. "TK, look, I'm sorry. I wanted to tell you, but I was scared," I whined.

TK didn't reply. He turned on the shower and started taking off his clothes.

"TK, I know you hear me! So, you gon' ignore me?"

"I'm listening, Kandi, go ahead and speak," TK uttered as he got in the shower.

I closed the toilet and sat down, trying to think of the right words to say. TK peeped his head out the shower curtain to make sure I was still there, then he pulled his head back in.

"So, are you going to talk or not?" TK asked with an attitude.

"Yes."

"Well talk then. I'm waiting."

"I never meant to hurt you at all, and the only reason didn't tell you is that I didn't want to see you hurt."

"If you knew this shit would hurt me, then why did you do it?"

"I don't know. I just got caught up in the moment, TK."

"You like that shit? She ate that pussy better than me?" he interrogated.

I can just imagine his face behind that shower curtain.

"Noh she didn't," I answered, rolling my eyes.

Blaze had some good ass tongue action, but she didn't have shit on TK at all, and his dick was the truth.

"Okay."

TK turned off the shower and got out. I handed him his dry off towel and walked into our bedroom. I got dressed in my pajamas and lay in the bed. TK did the same. The whole night, we didn't speak to each other at all. I even tried to suck his dick, but it wouldn't even get hard for me. TK must have been mad because every time I touch him, his dick gets hard. I pass out before TK; he was still up watching *Friday*.

TK

Truth is, I love my girl, but to hear her admit to what she did broke my heart. I'm madder at the fact that she lied to my face when I asked her had she slept with somebody when I was locked up. She told me no with no hesitation, and I believed her sneaky ass. I don't understand why she lied. We stayed in the strip club together before I got locked up. I knew she liked girls, but I didn't think she would take it that far and sleep with one, especially a stripper. Them hoes nasty, and they will do any and everything for a dollar. Just the thought of Kandi fucking this bitch made me sick to the stomach.

I'm still trying to figure out how could sleep with somebody her best friend was having an affair with on her man. I shook my head as I reached over to my nightstand and grabbed my phone. I put my password in and scrolled down to Kim's unsaved number. I made sure I threw that receipt away with Kim's name on it and saved it in my phone.

Me: What up?

Kim: Who is this?

Me: You give a nigga that good ass loving and forget me that quick? This TK.

Kim: Lol shut up! I don't have your number, so I didn't know who it was.

Me: Well you know now.

Kim: Lol what you doing?

Me: Nothing laying down thinking about your sexy ass.

Kim: Don't hype my head. Let me come lay with you.

Me: I wish you could.

Kim: Why can't I?

Me: Because my girl is laying next to me.

Kim: Girl??

Me: Yeah, girl.

Kim didn't reply to my text. I guess she was mad when I mentioned I had a girl.

Gee

When I got home, I took a hot shower and watched a couple of movies with Shannon and my lil baby. I can't lie, my guilt was eating me alive for fucking Kia. Every time Shannon's phone rang I got nervous. I thought it was Kia telling her that we had sex behind the gym in my car. I'm just hoping that Kia keep her mouth closed because I don't feel like fighting with Shannon's ass at all, and if Kia knew what was best for her, she would keep quiet on her end.

I love my wifey, but I keep having flashbacks of Kia sucking and fucking me. Every time I thought about it, my dick got hard. I made a vow to my wife that I would never cheat on her again. I feel bad for letting another woman satisfy me like she was my wife. Kia was worth it, though, because she fucked the shit out of me and her head game was on point.

"Baby, what you thinking about?" Shannon asked, quickly snapping me out my thoughts.

"Nothing, baby, just life."

"Oh."

I thought Shannon was going to go on and on with the questions, but she didn't. Probably because she was so into the movie she was watching on Lifetime.

Blaze

After I made it to my destination, I got myself settled in and called up my lil boo thang. I made sure I freshened up real good because ain't no telling what's going down when I hear that knock on the door. I couldn't wait to see my boo. I poured me up a shot of Goose and rolled a joint that I got before I made it to the hotel. I took my shot, and as soon as I was about to blaze my joint, there was a knock on the door. A smiled filled my face as I walked over to the door to open it. I stood there in my silk robe and red thong on with no bra.

"You look sexy, ma."

"Thank you. You don't look too bad yourself," I said, and we both laughed.

"I miss you."

"I miss you too, Blake."

I don't know what it was, but it was something about Kia that got my juices flowing just looking at her. I met Kia in the institute I was locked up in. She had already been there a year when I came. She had five months left when I came in. Kia had never messed with a woman. I was her first and her last. Kia was locked up because she stabbed her ex-boyfriend for cheating on her with the girl next door. Kia and I became close as time went by. When we got free time in the institute, we used to sneak off and have sex.

I told her the reason I was locked up, and Kia was pissed off. I told Kia I would pay her a couple of stacks if she helped me get revenge on Shannon and Gee. I had a couple of bands put up in my banking account for a rainy day. The plan was to get Shannon to get cool with Kia until I came home. I don't know what I was going to do with Shannon, but I was going to come up with a plan ASAP. I told Kia to do whatever it takes. I don't care if she has to eat her out. I trusted Kia, I knew she won't to let me down. Even though we haven't known each other that long, I could feel the connection between us.

Kia

Blake is cool and all, but I don't even like girls. Don't get me wrong, the sex between me and Blake was good, but she was just something to do while I was locked up. I got to admit I did gain lil feelings for Blake, but I was just going through a phase. Plus, I couldn't get no dick. Blake wanted me to set Shannon up, but now that I've met Shannon I'm having second thoughts. Shannon is real laid back and cool, but I can tell from her demeanor she will fuck a bitch up if crossed. Now that I'm free, I'm not trying to get involved with what Blake has going on. Plus, I think I'm feeling Gee.

Gee wasn't part of the plan at all. Shannon always talked about Gee and how good of a man he is, but I never met him until the other day when she introduced us at the gym. It was like love at first sight when I saw him. I don't think Gee felt the same way because he barely acknowledged me. I wasn't planning on messing around with Gee, but when I laid eyes on him, I couldn't help myself. He wasn't fine, but he had his own look. I'm just trying to get in where I fit in. I don't mind being the side chick as long as he plays by my rules. Not to mention, that D is the truth.

Gee

The next day when I got up, Shannon was getting dressed.

"Where you going?" I asked.

"I just have to run to a couple of stores and pick up some things for dinner," Shannon replied.

"I want you to be my dinner," I said jokingly.

"How about I be your dinner and your dessert?" Shannon said, rubbing her kitty. We both laughed.

"I will be back in about two hours. Oh yeah, Kia is supposed to stop by and drop off an outfit she bought the baby."

"Okay."

When Shannon said that Kia was coming over, my heart dropped. Kia knew damn well she wasn't coming over here to drop no outfit off. I just hoped she don't come over here trying to be on no bull. About twenty minutes after Shannon left, there was a knock on the door. A part of me didn't want to open the door because I didn't know if I could resist Kia.

"What up?" I said, standing in the doorway.

"Hey, I was just dropping off some things off for the baby."

Kia was looking good as hell. She had her hair pinned up into a bun with a red summer dress that hugged every inch of her body. She had on Chanel sandals with a French pedicure. I looked Kia up and down. My dick automatically got hard. I reached for the bag and was about to shut the door, but Kia put her foot in the way.

"You're not going to invite me in?" Kia asked, giving me a seductive look.

She leaned in and placed a kiss on my lips. I couldn't help but kiss her back. I picked Kia up and wrap her legs around my waist and her arms around my neck. We continued to kiss until I made it to the couch and laid her down. I walked back over to the door and locked it. When I made in back over to Kia, she had her legs wide open. I knew Kia came over here to get this because she didn't have no panties on. I began to kiss all over the inside of her thighs, and I slipped my index finger inside her. Kia's pussy was so warm and wet. I pulled down my boxers and Atlanta Falcons pajama pants. I slid my long, thick log inside of her.

"Umm," she groaned as soon as I entered her.

I don't know what it is, but I can't seem to resist Kia's ass. I'm surprised I even got hard because I fucked the shit out of Shannon last night. Soon as I got all into it, my baby began to cry.

"Shit," I said, pulling out of Kia and putting my clothes back on.

"Damn, so you just going to stop fucking me?"

"Yeah, don't you hear my baby crying?"

"She can't wait?" she questioned.

"Hell naw, but you can."

I went upstairs, leaving Kia on the couch. I put some sanitizer on my hands and grabbed my baby out the baby bed.

"Hey, Daddy baby," I whispered, staring into my baby's eyes.

When I looked at my baby, I saw Shannon. They looked just alike. I couldn't help but smile every time I saw my daughter's face or heard her little voice. Kia had me messed up if she thought I was about to keep fucking her while my baby was crying. That shit turned me off real fast. After sitting there staring at my baby and how beautiful she was, I went downstairs and told Kia she had to go. She had a little attitude, but I didn't care. I had to attend to my damn baby. Soon as Kia was walking out the door, Kandi was standing right there.

"Where Shannon at?" Kandi questioned, looking Kia up and down.

"She ain't here," Kia replied with a sneaky grin on her face.

"Bitch, was I talking to you, hoe?" Kandi shouted.

"Naw, bitch, but I'm talking to you."

"You can't be talking to me, bitch, why are you even here? Shannon is gone."

"Shannon knows why I'm here," Kia stated.

"Well, you need to be leaving. For all I know, you can be trying to fuck her husband."

Kia smiled and replied, "Girl, bye. Move out my way."

She tried to push her way through Kandi, and before I knew it, Kandi had punched Kia in her face, and they were banging. I hurried up and laid my baby's blanket down on the floor and laid her down. I ran over there and tried to pull Kandi off Kia, but she wasn't letting go.

"Bitch, didn't I say I wasn't talking to your dumb ass?" Kandi shouted as she punched Kia.

"Let her go, Kandi," I demanded.

"Nope, fuck this bitch. She thinks she hard! I'ma show her ass today."

I finally got them apart, and Kandi was trying her best to attack Kia, but I held her tight. Kia ran out the door and left. I don't know what the beef is between Kia and Kandi, but I can tell they already been beefing. If Kia knew better, she would've kept her mouth shut when it came to Kandi because her ass doesn't have no sense when she's mad. I got to say, Kandi can fight her ass off to be little, and she don't take no shit from nobody. After about twenty minutes, I finally got her to calm down, and Shannon walked in.

Blake

When Kia came over to see me, she was acting kind of weird. I wanted to follow her ass when she left, but I was waiting for my cousin to drop my car off. I let my cousin use my car while I was locked up. I didn't have a use for it, and she had three kids. She finally brought my car later that night. The next day I called Kia to see where she was, and she told me she was on her way to Shannon's house. They were going to the gym. I took it upon myself to post up and watch Shannon's house since Kia was acting kind of fishy yesterday. She was acting like she was happy to see me, but every time I tried to get a taste, she pushed me away and made up some bogus ass excuse.

I saw Shannon leave and get in her car. It took all of me not to get out the car and snatch Shannon up. She was looking extra good, and I wanted her right then and there. I pulled myself together because I could feel my body taking over my mind. You know how they say a nigga think with they dick? Well, I was thinking with my pussy when I saw Shannon's thick ass. I snapped out of my thoughts and pulled myself together.

About twenty minutes later, Kia pulled up. She walked up to the door with a gift bag and Gee open it. Next thing I knew, she was tonguing this nigga down, and she was loving that shit. I can't lie, I was mad as hell. I wanted to get out and snatch her ass away from him, but I just watched and took a picture on my cell phone. If this was me a year ago, it would've been a problem, no lie. I had to learn and work on my patience. That's how I got caught up last time, being thirsty and not paying attention. I took pictures as Gee carried Kia into the house. I had no doubt in my mind that they were making love to each other. The way they were kissing and how he grabbed that ass when he picked her up. There is no uncertainty that they have fucked before. They looked too comfortable with each other.

Since Kia wanted to play games, I'm going to show her how to play games. I left soon as Kia went in the house with Gee. I called Kia a couple of time while she was in the house, but she didn't answer.

Kandi

After I beat Kia's ass, I have to say I felt way better. I already had so much anger built up in me from the situation me and TK were going through, and Kia had the nerve to put that grimy smirk on her face. That's why I smacked it right off. If I find out that she crossed the line with Gee, it's going to be hell to pay. I don't like sneaky bitches at all.

When I got up this morning, there were no words between me and TK. He got up, looked at his phone, and left. Usually, he would eat breakfast, but he just left without saying a word. I know what I did was wrong, but damn, it ain't like I fucked another man. I'm not justifying what I did with Blake because she's a female, I just didn't think he would take as badly as he did. I could only imagine how he would act if it were another man who had me. After TK left, I called up Shannon, but her phone kept going to her voicemail. I got dressed and headed over to Shannon's house because I needed to vent.

After me and Kia finished fighting, Shannon came home about five minutes later. I was pacing the floor with my hand on my hips when she walked in.

"What's wrong with you?" Shannon asked, dropping all her bags at the door and rushing over to me.

"That bitch Kia is what's wrong with me," I replied.

"Really, Kandi? You letting her get to you like that? I thought something was really wrong," Shannon barked and start walking away.

"Something is wrong! That bitch was in the house with your husband."

"Kandi, I knew she was coming."

"Yeah, that bitch was cumming alright," I said in a sarcastic way.

"What's that supposed to mean?"

"Ask your husband."

Gee looked at me nervously while holding the baby.

"Gee, what she talking about?" Shannon questioned crossing her arm over her chest.

I didn't know if Gee fucked Kia, but I had a good hunch he did by the way she was acting.

"I... I don't know," Gee stuttered.

"I bet he don't," I stated. "You know what? I don't have time for this bullshit. I got enough problems of my own," I proclaimed and walked out the door.

Gee was sitting there stuttering like he was being questioned by the cops. I could tell by how nervous Gee was that he was lying straight through his teeth. When I got in my car, I called TK's phone, but I didn't get no answer. I don't understand why TK was acting like it's the end of the world. I understand I lied, but to be treating me like he doesn't love me anymore is killing me softly.

I stopped at the liquor store, grabbed me a bottle of goose, and pulled up to my house ten minutes later. When I walked in, TK was on the phone. Whoever he was talking to, he told them he will call them back later.

"Who was that?" I asked.

"Nobody."

"Somebody. You weren't talking to yourself, TK."

"Don't come in here starting with me, Kandi."

"Well, if you start acting like my man instead of my enemy, I wouldn't have to start with your ass," I said, walking to the kitchen and pouring me some wine.

TK followed me. "Oh, was I your man when you had your legs open to that bitch Blaze?" he shouted and took a pull from his joint.

"You know what, you acting real childish. Why you can't just talk to me like a man instead of acting like a bitch?"

TK walked over to me, pointed his hand in my face, and said, "Call me another bitch and I'ma smack fire out your ass."

I looked at TK with fear in my eyes.

"Yeah, that's what I thought," TK said as he stood there smoking his joint.

I didn't have anything else to say. I just broke down and started crying. Deep down inside I wanted to get a knife and slice his throat. But, I knew I had no chance with TK. I could see TK staring at me out the corner of his eyes.

"Come here, don't cry. I'm sorry," TK exclaimed, holding his arms open.

I walked over to him and laid my head on his shoulder. Knowing that he still cared melted my heart. TK rubbed my back, giving me comfort as he whispered, *I'm sorry* repeatedly in my ear.

"I love you, TK, I'm sorry for not telling you," I sobbed as tears flowed down my face.

"Baby, I'm sorry for acting like an asshole. Just the thought of somebody else getting between your thighs drove me crazy," he responded, sounding sincere.

I sniffled and lifted my head off his shoulder. "I promise it won't happen again, baby."

"Shhh, it's okay," TK said as he rubbed his hands through my hair.

He grabbed my hand and walked me into the living room. Next, he laid me on the couch and placed his soft lips on mine. Then he took my clothes off until I was completely naked. He turned me over on my stomach and started massaging my shoulders. He then worked his way down to my ass cheeks and started massaging them. My pussy got wet immediately.

"Umm," I groaned from the touch of his hands massaging my body.

Next, he began to kiss me down my spine, making chills shoot through my body. TK got up and took his clothes off and told me to scoot to the end of the couch. He knelt before me and started eating that pussy like he hadn't had a meal in years. I squirmed around as soon as his tongue met my clit.

"Un un, stop moving. Let me eat that pussy," TK demanded as he lifted his face up from my juices and then plunged his face right back in it.

That tongue was feeling so good, I couldn't help but move up and down on his face. After TK ate my pussy for about twenty minutes, he commanded me to give him some head. He got from between my thighs and sat next to me. I got off the couch and dropped to my knees right in front of TK. I grabbed his already hard dick with my right hand and his balls with my left one. I licked all over his dick until it was completely wet. I jerked his dick back and forth while my tongue licked his dick head. TK wrapped my hair around his hand and motioned my head to move back and forth.

"You sucking the shit out that dick," TK expressed as his head leaned back and his eyes closed.

I could feel his dick getting harder and harder by the second.

"Lean over the couch. I'm ready to do some damage to that pussy," TK expressed as he stood there jacking his dick slowly, waiting for me to get into position. He positioned his hands on my little waistline and jammed his big long log inside of me.

"I love my pussy. I'm sorry, I'm sorry, baby," he repeated, hitting my pussy harder every time.

I loved when TK talked to me during sex. It made me super wet.

"Hit it harder," I ordered, exploding all over his dick.

Before I knew it, TK was cumming all over my ass. TK fell to one knee right after he nutted, that's how you know that sex was good.

Shannon

I don't know what I just walked into, but I'm hoping what Kandi told me isn't true.

"What was that all about?"

"I don't know. Kandi tripping," Gee replied nervously.

"Is she?" I asked.

"Look, Kandi came over here when Kia was walking out the door. They had words, and one thing led to another," Gee explained to me.

"Okay, so why do Kandi think y'all fucked?"

"I don't know. Maybe because she don't like the girl! Maybe because she wants you to fall out with Kia," Gee said.

"That's just not making sense to me."

"I don't care if it ain't making no sense. Ain't shit happen," Gee justified as he fed the baby.

"Well, I'm just going to give Kia a call and see what's going on, so all this nonsense can stop," I stated and reach for my phone out of my Michael Kors clutch.

I scrolled down my contacts to Kia's number, and as soon as I was about to press call, a message came in. I went to the message, and it was a picture from a number I've never seen before. I opened the picture and Gee was holding Kia and kissing her. I couldn't believe my eyes.

"So, you don't know what the fuck Kandi talking about?" I shouted, pointing my finger in Gee's face.

"Chill out, my baby just went to sleep. Let me lay her down." Gee walked upstairs and laid our baby down then came back down.

"Shannon, I didn't touch that bitch."

Tears filled the rim of my eye as I stared at Gee with rage in my eyes.

"Gee, stop lying to me!" I shouted to the top of my lungs.

"I'm not lying."

"If you didn't fuck her what is this?" I shove my phone in Gee's face.

He took it out my hand and stared at the picture in shock. "Shannon, baby, I can explain."

"Explain what that you been fucking this bitch in our house."

"Shannon I swear I only fucked her here once." Gee clarified like that mattered.

"Oh, so you fucked her more than once? How many times has it been?" I questioned.

I stood there with my arms crossed over my chest.

"Twice."

"Twice! You fucked this bitch twice! Gee oh my god." I snatched my cell phone out of Gee's hand and headed for the door.

Gee followed behind me and grabbed me "Shannon just listen to me please." Gee pleaded.

"Listen to what?"

"I listened to you when you cheated on me with Blaze's ass."

"Oh, so is this what this is about?" I asked as I wrestled my way out of Gee's arms and looked him in his eyes.

"No, but I want you to listen to me," Gee replied.

"Go ahead talk." I barked standing there with my hands on my hip.

"She came on to me, baby. That girl don't mean shit to me, it just happened."

"Oh, it just happened, huh?" I yelled, and before I knew it, I smacked the shit out of Gee,

I could tell it took all of Gee not to put his hands on me. He grabbed me and threw me down on the couch.

"Man, I said I'm sorry damn you don't forgive me."

I couldn't believe that Gee cheated on me with Kia she ain't even all that. He could've at least fuck somebody that was topping me. I guess Kandi was right about Kia. I wish I would've just listened to Kandi, but I was giving Kia the benefit of the doubt. I can't wait to talk to Kandi to let her know that this bitch is everything she said she was.

After talking to Gee for about thirty minutes I finally forgave him, but just because I forgave him don't mean I'm going to forget. Gee sounded remorseful, and he promised me it won't happen again. I believe him for some reason. I still feel bad for what I did to Gee when I cheated with Blaze, that's why it was easy for me to forgive him. I guess the guilt from what I did to Gee was still eating me alive.

After me and Gee finished talking, I hit up Kandi to let her know that what she said was true. Of course, she was ready to fight. Kandi told me to get dressed, and she was on her way. I went into my walk-in closet and grabbed my black and white Nike sweat suit and put on my all white Air Force Ones. I pulled my hair back in a ponytail and got dressed. I sat on the couch and waited for Kandi to pull up.

Gee already knew what I was about to do. I could tell Gee didn't want me to go, but he knew he wasn't talking me out of this one. Plus, he knows he messed up. Usually, I wouldn't be fighting, especially since I got a baby, but Kia got to get her ass whooped for this one. She thinks Kandi beat her ass, but she hasn't felt my wrath yet. I was still trying to figure out who sent me the picture. Every time I called the number, I got no answer. I even texted it a couple of times asking who it was.

Finally, I heard Kandi blowing her horn, and I left.

Blaze

After Kia betrayed me, I sent the picture of her and Gee to Shannon. I know right about now Shannon is either beating Kia ass or on her way to beat her ass. Shannon texted me a couple of times asking who I was, but I didn't reply. I'm trying to figure out how I can kidnap Shannon. Then it dawned on me, and I had a plan. I finally returned Shannon's text, but I didn't tell her who I was. I just let her know that I had more information about Gee's infidelities, and if she wanted the truth about her man to meet me at 5555 Kirkwood Drive tonight at 8:00 pm, use the back door, and come alone. She texted back and said she will be there. Kirkwood is an abandoned house, but it doesn't look abandoned on the inside.

On the outside, the windows are boarded up, but on the inside, it's nice. This is where O Dog used to keep his drugs. He had it laid out in there like it was his house. A queen size bed in the bedroom for when he used to trap, a living room set, and two flat screen TVs. O Dog used to pay the owner rent just to trap out of it, but he told the owner that he wanted to keep the window boarded up so it would look abandoned. I'm quite sure the owner knew what O Dog was doing in his house, but he didn't care because of the amount of money he was getting. I got myself together to get everything prepared for when Shannon comes. It was already a quarter after five.

The thought of Shannon in my presence sent butterflies through my stomach. I don't know if I'm going to have the balls to torture her or kill her. Just her name itself make me weak for her. I just want to make love to her one more time. I can taste her juices on my tongue as I reminisce about her. I just wish Shannon would leave Gee's ass, but after I get Shannon, Gee is next.

Shannon

We pulled up to the gym where me and Kia work out. I hoped that Kia was still at the gym because she usually leaves at about five thirty when she goes alone, and it was almost six o'clock. We pulled to the back of the gym where Kia parked, and as soon as we pulled up, Kia was coming out. I told Kandi to stay in the car for now because I didn't want Kia to see her and get scared. Thank God Kandi's car had tint on it.

"Kia, can I talk to you for a second?" I asked as I approached Kia. I could tell she was kind of nervous.

"Sure, Shannon, what's up?" Kia answered.

"So, what went on between you and Kandi?"

"Well, she started tripping when she saw me dropping the gifts off for your baby. She starts getting smart and questioning why was I in your house when you wasn't there," Kia explained in a shaky voice.

"Why would you be in my house? Why didn't you just hand it to him and leave?"

Kia took a minute to reply like she was thinking of an answer.

"Because I had to use the restroom, and Gee said I can come in," she replied, looking at me with fear in her eyes.

"It's three things I hate. A liar, thief, and a back stabber. How many times you fucked my husband?" I interrogated Kia.

"What? I didn't fuck him."

"Gee already told me the truth, so stop lying bitch!"

"Shannon, it only happened a couple of times. I'm sorry, I never meant—"

Before Kia could get the rest of her words out, I smacked the shit out of her ass. I smacked her so hard she stumbled to the ground. I heard a car door shut and Kandi ran up, ready to attack. I didn't even get a chance to touch Kia again. Kandi pulled Kia by her hair and was dragging her and punching her in the face.

"Bitch, don't ever disrespect my friend, hoe," Kandi shouted as she continually punched Kia in her face.

Kia's face was bloody, and I had to pull Kandi off her before she killed her. I finally got Kandi to let her hair go, and Kia was just lying there barely moving. Me and Kandi hurried up and ran to the car and pulled off. I saw Kia trying to get up as we left. I got a feeling that Kia going to retaliate after getting her ass whoop twice in one day.

I arrived back at my house around seven fifteen, and when I got there, Gee was passed out. I didn't bother to wake him up because I was about to leave back out. I had received a text back from the person who sent me the pictures. The person claimed they had more info about Gee cheating on me. If I find out he's been doing more than what he said, it's going to be a big problem. Plus, I want to know who is behind these messages. I grabbed my keys and was on my way to 5555 Kirkwood Drive.

Kia

These bitches had another thing coming if they thought they were going to get away with what they did to me. When I made it home, I washed my face and got in the shower because I had blood everywhere. I had a busted lip, nose, and my right eye was turning black. After I got out the shower, I hit up Blaze and told her that I wanted to get in on the plan. She told me to go and kill Gee. I would have thought she would've said kill Shannon, but I guess she wants her all to herself. I told Blaze I was down for whatever. She explained to me that Shannon was on the way to meet her and I needed to get to Shannon's house ASAP. I told her I would be there in half an hour. Even though my body was sore, I was still going to make my way to Shannon's house.

Since she and her friend wanted to hurt me, so I'm going to teach her ass a lesson. She's going to hurt worse than I was. I grabbed the gun that belonged to my boyfriend out of the top drawer and left. The whole way to Gee's house, I imagined myself killing him. Gee didn't have anything to do with what Kandi and Shannon did, but I know if I kill him, Shannon will be devastated. I didn't want to take Gee away from his child because my father was taken away from me when I was little. I pulled up to Gee and Shannon's house and got out the car. My heart was pounding fast, and I was nervous. I've never killed anyone a day in my life. Hell, I never even used a gun.

I walked up to the front door and knocked a couple of times, but I didn't get an answer. I had the gun in my right hand behind my back. I knocked again, but still no answer. As soon as I was about to walk away, Gee answered the door.

"Kia, what you doing here? Look, I have to leave you alone. Shannon knows."

Just hearing Gee saying those words pissed me clean the fuck off. I reached behind my back and aimed the gun at Gee. He put both of his hands up, and said, "Bitch, if you shoot me you better kill me."

Before I knew it, I fired two shots, and Gee was on the ground. I ran to my car and sped off. I knew for sure that Gee was dead because he wasn't moving at all when I looked back.

Kandi

I made it back home, and when I walked in, TK's phone was ringing. He was knocked out on the recliner chair in our living room. I called his name to let him know that his phone was ringing, but he didn't move at all. He must have been super high or drunk. By the time I reached for the phone, it stopped ringing. Before I could walk away, it started ringing again. I picked the phone up off his lap and answered it.

"Hello."

"Who is this?" a woman voice questioned.

"You called my man's phone, so the only person should be asking questions is me," I proclaimed with an attitude.

"Ha-ha, girl put our man on the phone." She laughed, thinking this shit was a joke.

"Bitch, I will beat your ass. You better ask about me."

"Girl, I already know about you. I see why TK cheating on your ratchet ass, just listen to you."

"Where you stay at?" I asked.

"Ask our man, he knows."

"Bitch, oh you want to be sarcastic, but I bet this shit don't be funny when I'm in your face."

"Ha-ha. Tell TK I called."

"Naw, hold on."

"TK, wake up!" I yelled as I shook him.

"What's up, baby? Why you yelling?" TK asked.

"Phone," I said and crossed my arms over my chest.

I could tell from the look on TK's face that he knew exactly who was on the phone.

"Who is it?" TK questioned as he reached for the phone.

He hesitated to get on the phone, then he finally said hello. I could hear her on the other end.

"So, you got that bitch answering your phone now?"

"Man, chill out," TK replied.

"Naw, you chill out. Tell that bitch don't answer your phone when she sees my number."

"Man, this my phone. Don't tell me what the fuck to do," TK stated.

"So, who the fuck is she, TK?" I butted into the conversation.

"Nobody," TK replied.

"Obviously, somebody," I responded and punched him in his chest.

TK just looked at me crazy because he knew what he did was wrong.

"Man, this bitch ain't nobody."

"Bitch? Oh, I'm a bitch now? I wasn't a bitch when you were all in these guts," the girl yelled.

"Look, fuck it. I'm busted now. Kandi, this bitch doesn't mean shit to me. I was just mad at you, and she came on to me, and one thing led to another."

"So, you fucked this nasty bitch to get back at me?"

"I did it out of anger. It won't happen again. I apologize," TK uttered.

"Man, fuck that bitch, TK," the girl shouted through the phone."

"Naw, bitch, it's fuck you," TK defended me and hung up.

This explains why TK had been acting so differently toward me. This nigga been having an affair, and ain't no telling how long this shit has been going on. At this point, I had nothing to say to TK because I wasn't in the right state of mind. I could kill TK right now.

"I'm sorry, Kandi."

"I don't want to hear that bullshit at all! If you think fucking another woman is going to solve our problems, you're wrong," I yelled as I mushed TK's head back.

I knew for a fact that if TK hit me back, I was going to be knocked out, but I didn't give a fuck. I was mad. I felt like I could beat the world. My cell phone began to ring, interrupting me and TK's argument. I wasn't going to answer it because me and TK had some unfinished business, but I saw that it was Shannon calling. Anything could be wrong, especially after I just beat the hell out of Kia's ass.

"Hello."

"Kandi, if you don't hear from me in ten minutes, call me," Shannon whispered.

"What you mean? Are you okay, Shannon?"

"I'm here on Kirk…"

Shannon's phone began to break up, and I couldn't hear a word she was saying.

"Hello," I repeated several times.

I looked at my phone and noticed that our call was disconnected.

"Is everything okay, baby?" TK asked.

"No, I think something is wrong with Shannon," I replied.

"What you mean?"

"I will explain everything on the way to Shannon's house. Let's go," I demanded as I rushed to the door.

"Hold on, let me grab my pistol," TK said.

Shannon

Soon as I pulled up to 5555 Kirkwood Drive, I got a funny feeling in my stomach. Something was telling me to turn around and leave. The house was nice, but the windows were boarded up. I got out my car and put my cell phone in my jacket pocket. I walked to the back of the house. The closer I got to the back door, the more nervous I became. I approached the back door, and it was already cracked open. My heart was telling me to leave, but my mind was telling me to stay and see what this person had to tell me about my husband.

I knocked on the door, and it opened even more. I stuck my head in to see if I saw anyone. I walked in slowly, looking around to make sure that the coast was clear. When I got in, I was standing in the kitchen. From the kitchen, I could see the living room. It looked like a candle was lit because I could see some type of light reflecting off the wall. Soon as I walked close to the living, the back door slammed, scaring the shit out of me.

"So, finally, we meet again."

I knew that voice anywhere, and when I heard it, my heart dropped. Blaze turned on the light in the kitchen. She had her hair pulled up in a bun, and she was standing there in a sexy bra and panty set. I didn't know if I should run or kiss her. I couldn't deny it, Blaze was looking real delicious. Blaze walked over to me and stood in front of me. Before I knew it, we were kissing for about five minutes. I know what I was doing right now was wrong, but it felt so good. Once again, I had fallen into Blaze's love spell.

Blaze began licking and kissing me on my neck. She started removing my clothes off my hot and ready body. After she removed my clothes, I removed hers. Blaze got on her knees and licked me from my calves all the way up to my pussy. When she reached my pussy, she kissed all around it. Opening my legs a little wider, she then stuck her tongue in my pussy hole and tongue fucked me. I gripped her hair as I moaned repetitively from the feeling. Blaze got up, grabbed my hand, and led me to the bedroom. I lay down on the bed and put my hand behind my head.

"Naw, get up. I want you doggy style," Blaze commanded.

I got in the doggy style position, placing a deep arch in my back. I buried my face in the pillow that was on the bed. Blaze took both her hands, separated my ass cheeks, and began to lick my ass. The shit was feeling so good I gripped the pillow. I slid my hand under the pillow and gripped the sheets, only to feel a pistol. I played it off. Blaze either had that gun there for protection or to kill me. Blaze ate my ass for at least five minutes. Next, she told me to lay on my back she dived her face right into my kitty, wasting no time. She plunged her middle finger into me as her lips clenched my clit. Blaze sucked on it slowly, making my clit get hard. Blaze had the best the head ever. I could feel my nut building up, and it was only seconds before I blasted all over Blaze's face. My clit began to get sensitive the more Blaze sucked it. Blaze knew exactly when to suck it and when to lick it. Seconds later, my pussy started to release all my fluids.

"Awwwwww, fuck! Umm umm, eat that pussy," I moaned as Blaze fingered and sucked my clit.

I was breathing heavily and still moaning. Blaze got up from between my legs and stood up. I told her to face the wall and put her hand on the wall. Of course, she followed my demand. I slid the pistol from under the pillow and laid it on the bed, making sure I covered it with the cover. I got off the bed and stood behind Blaze and started hugging her from the back. I gripped her juicy breasts and kissed her neck. I removed my hand from around her and gripped her juicy fat ass. It was so soft, I didn't want to let it go.

"Stay just like this, baby," I whispered in Blaze's ear and licked it.

"Okay, I will do whatever you want me to do," Blaze responded.

I walked over to the bed and grabbed the pistol from under the cover. I aimed at the back of Blaze's head.

"Blaze, I just want to say thank you for letting me bust on your face like the whore you are."

Blaze turned around to a pistol in her face.

"Oh, you going to shoot me, Shannon?"

"Naw, bitch, I'm going to kill your ass," I stated and shot Blaze in the head.

I watched her body hit the floor, and blood splattered everywhere. Thank God, the gun had a silencer on it. I ran into the kitchen, put my clothes on, and then ran to my car. I opened the trunk and grabbed my gasoline can. I only had a little gasoline in it. I went back into the house, grabbed the candle out of the living room, and walked back into the bedroom. Blaze was still was lying there in a puddle of blood. I poured gasoline all over the bed and then all over Blaze. I set the candle on the floor and stuck the end of the sheet into the candle. I walked outside the room as I watched it go up in flames. I moved quickly out the door, got in my car, and zoomed off.

Kia

On the way back home, I had to hit my girl Kim up to let her know what's been going on between me, Shannon and Kandi. Since she had been fucking with TK for a couple of weeks, I'm quite sure she wouldn't mind hearing this tea. After I tell Kim, I know she going to be ready to fight. Soon as I got ready to dial Kim's number she called me.

"Girl, I was just about to call you—"

"Girlllll, let me tell you! Why I call TK's phone and that bitch Kandi answered," Kim shouted through the phone cutting me off before I could finish.

"What! What happened?"

"She just started talking mad shit like she was hard. I kept saying our man, making her mad. Where you at, I got to come to see you and tell you the story."

"I'm about to pull up in about ten minutes. Meet me there because I got to tell you what happened today," I replied.

"Okay, I'm close to your house now. I might beat you there."

"Okay."

I couldn't wait to make it home so I could tell Kim what happened, and I damn sure couldn't wait to see what Kim had to tell me. I wasn't going to tell Kim I killed Gee because I'm not trying to do no time, and she might slip up and tell somebody. I pulled into my driveway about ten minutes later, and Kim was waiting by my door. I took my key out the ignition and walked to the door.

"Bitch, what the fuck happened to you face?" Kim yelled as I unlocked my house door.

"Girl, that's what I got to tell you."

Kim knew that I wanted Gee, but I didn't tell her we fucked. I told her we only flirted with each other and hugged. I was going to tell her, but I was waiting until I got in good with Gee, but that got messed up. I had my eyes on TK before. Thank God I didn't talk to him because Kandi is a crazy ratchet bitch.

"Well, first off, I been fucking Gee."

"What? Are you serious?" Kim replied with a shocked look on her face.

"Yeah, I'm serious, but to make a long story short, Kandi came over when I was leaving, and we started fighting. Later that day, I hit the gym to relieve some anger, and Shannon popped up as I was leaving out," I explained.

"What! So, what happened next?" Kim questioned, sitting on the edge of the couch.

"Well, Shannon approached me and questioned me about my and Gee's affair. I denied it, but she said Gee had already told her. Next thing I know, this bitch slapped me off guard, and I fell to the ground. Then, out of nowhere, Kandi ran up, and we started fighting again."

"So these hoes jumped you? Oh, hell naw let's go whoop they ass." Kim stood up, ready to fight.

"No, it's cool. I got it under control."

"Look at your face. You call that under control?" Kim said, standing there with her hands on her hips.

"Kim, it's cool. Trust me."

"Newsflash, why should I trust you when you standing here with a black eye, busted lip, and a swollen face? We should be stomping them hoes faces in the ground right about now," Kim said as she looked at her watch.

After about twenty minutes, I finally got Kim to calm down, even though I could tell she was still pissed off. I was mad about what happened to me, but when Shannon finds out her man is dead, that's going to hurt worse.

"What happened between you Kandi over the phone."

"Well, I called to talk to TK and Kandi answered. I was like who is this? And Kandi gon' say, 'you called my man's phone. I'm the only one who should be asking questions.'"

"Ha-ha, she meant y'all man," I said, interrupting Kim.

We both laughed.

"I said, girl, put our man on the phone. When I said that, Kandi got pissed off. She started screaming I will beat your ass and all that nonsense."

We both chuckled again.

"Yeah, Kandi thinks she can't be touched or something," I said.

"Well, she got the right bitch. But, anyway, she started screaming for TK to wake up. She finally got him, and he basically started trying to dog me like I wasn't shit. I mean, I know we only fucked like five times, but don't try to play me. He was telling me he was tired of Kandi and he don't love her like he used to because she did some scandalous shit," Kim stated.

"I wonder what she did," I replied.

"Me too. Whatever it was, I could tell it had TK heated."

"Her nasty ass probably fucked Gee too." We both laughed out loud.

Me and Kim talked for a little while longer then she left. I took two shots of Patron, so I could get what I did to Gee off my mind. Half an hour later, I was still awake. I got up and grabbed the Patron bottle and took it to the face. Before I knew it, I passed out.

Kandi

On the way to Shannon and Gee's house, my heart was racing. I had a funny feeling in my gut. I called Shannon's phone back several times. Me and TK even called Gee's phone, but we didn't get an answer. It's not like either of them not to answer at all or return our call. I hit a hundred miles per hour all the way to Shannon's house. When we pulled up, their house door was wide open.

TK hopped out the car before I could completely stop and park. TK ran in the house, and I ran behind him. When I made it to the door, I saw a trail of blood from the door to the couch, and Gee was just lying there.

"What the fuck? Brah, who did this shit? Baby, call 911 and go get some towels," TK yelled as he ran over to Gee.

I called 911 as I ran to the bathroom to grab the towels. I can't believe Gee was still breathing. He lost a ton of blood. We literally were sliding in it when we came through the door.

"That bitch shot me," Gee said, breathing heavily.

"What bitch?" TK asked as he put pressure on Gee's wound to his chest.

"Kia," Gee replied then he passed out.

"Gee, get up, brah," TK yelled as tears ran down his face.

I ran upstairs to check on the baby. I was in so much shock when I saw Gee that I forgot about her. When I arrived in her nursery, she was sleeping peacefully. I wrapped her blanket around her and lifted her out the bed slowly, making sure not to wake her. I could hear the sirens from the ambulance getting closer. About time I made it back downstairs, the paramedics were rushing in.

They checked Gee's pulse, lifted him off the floor, and rushed him to the ambulance. I started having flashbacks to when Shannon was shot. TK was standing there in devastation with tears covering his face. The police questioned us and asked us to leave because they needed to investigate. TK grabbed the car seat from by the door, and we walked out to my car. I put the baby in the car seat, and I realized I didn't have any diapers or milk. I walked back up to the door and asked the police if it would be okay if I grabbed some belongings for the baby. He told me, yes, but he made sure he trailed behind me. After I had what I needed, I got in to the car, put it in drive, and headed to the hospital.

Shannon

As I zoomed off, I reached into my pocket and grabbed my phone. I had twenty missed calls from Kandi, and twenty from TK. I knew something had to be wrong. I quickly dialed Kandi's number.

"Shannon, where the hell you been?" Kandi yelled as she answered the phone.

"Girl, long story. We need to talk asap," I responded.

"Shannon, I got some bad news."

"What, Kandi? What happened?" My heart was pounding so hard. I didn't know what Kandi was about to tell me.

"It's Gee."

"What you mean it's Gee! What happened? Where is my baby?" I screamed.

"We found him shot in y'all house. Your baby is in the car with us. She is fine."

"What! Oh my God, is he okay? Is he alive?"

"Yes, he was alive when we got there, but he passed out, and the ambulance came. So I don't know what's going on now."

"Was he talking when you got there? Did he say who did it?"

"Yes, and he said it was Kia," Kandi sobbed.

"Kia! That bitch, oh she got it coming," I replied with anger in my voice. I had to pull over, I was so pissed off.

"Yeah, she definitely signed her death certificate, but we on the way to Grady hospital now," Kandi stated.

"Okay, I will meet you there. I got to tell you what happened."

"Okay, see you in a minute, Shannon."

On the way to the hospital, all I could do was cry. I couldn't believe that Gee had been shot, and it is all my fault, once again. If I would've just stayed at home instead of trying to see what this person had to tell me, Gee wouldn't be in the hospital. I don't know if I'm cursed or what. It seemed like I've had the worse luck this past year. I got shot, Gee cheated, I killed Blaze after I let her taste me one last time, and now Gee is laying up in the hospital with bullets wounds in him, all because of me.

If would've never cheated, Gee wouldn't have cheated with Kia. Kia, on the other hand, is going to get dealt with ASAP. She's lucky Chaos is locked up, or he would be at her door right now. I really miss Chaos. He got locked up a couple of months ago for trafficking drugs. I write him every week and drop money on his books. When he finds out what happened to Gee, he is going to lose his mind. Kia thinks she going to get away with shooting Gee, but she got another thing coming. I know one thing for sure and two things for certain, if Gees dies, she might as well go dig her own grave.

I made it to the hospital and pulled into the parking garage. I put the car in park and removed the keys from the ignition. I bowed my head and began to pray. When I was finished, I got out the car, turned on my alarm, and walked to the elevators. When the elevators doors opened, Kandi, TK, and my baby were sitting in the waiting room. TK had blood all over his clothes, hands, and his eyes were bloodshot red. I could tell that TK had been crying the whole time. TK's eyes were so swollen from crying, I don't see how he was holding them open.

"Have y'all heard anything?" I asked rushing over to Kandi."

"No, we haven't heard anything," Kandi replied with a sad face.

I walked over to the help desk to see what was going on with Gee.

"Excuse me, can you give me some information on Gee Hightower?"

"Maybe," the nurse said with a stinking ass attitude.

"Maybe you need to do your job or find somebody else that will," I replied and rolled my eyes at the nurse.

The nurse looked at me with a snobby look on her face and began to check her computer.

"Mr. Hightower is in surgery right now. I will let the doctor know that his family is here," the nurse replied.

I nodded my head and walked away. I really wanted to grab her by her neck and bang her head repeatedly into the desk. That nurse had a fly ass mouth, and she had the right one tonight. If she doesn't like her job, she needs to quit like now. Because she got the right one on the wrong day. I wouldn't mind putting a bullet through her skull right about now. I went over and sat next to Kandi then reached for my baby. All I could do was hold her tightly and pray. She looked just like her daddy, but some people say she looks like me also. We had waited for about two hours before the doctor came out.

"Family for Mr. Hightower," the doctor called out.

"Right here. Is he okay?" I asked as I got up.

"Well, he lost a lot of blood and sustained a pretty severe head injury, which we believe happened when he fell after he was shot. Right now, he is still unconscious and the next twenty-four hours will be critical. He has about a 50/50 chance of survival at this time."

"Oh God," I said and fell to my knees.

The doctor grabbed my arm and pulled me off the floor.

"Ma'am, I know it's hard, but you need to be strong for Mr. Hightower," the doctor explained as he patted me on my shoulder.

"Can we see him?" I asked as tears filled the rim of my eyes.

"He's still in recovery, and we don't know when he'll wake up, but it's bot likely to be tonight. If you guys can come back tomorrow, that will be excellent," the doctor explained.

"Okay, what time are visiting hours?" I probed.

"From 7 a.m. until 8:30 p.m. for immediate family," the doctor answered.

"Okay."

The doctor told me if I had any questions to feel free to cal, and walked away.

I know one thing, I was not going home tonight without Gee. It just didn't feel right. I asked Kandi if I could stay at her house for a couple of days and she told me I could. I followed them as we drove down I-75. I couldn't wait to make it to Kandi's house so I could let her know what went down with Blaze. The whole time I was driving, all I could think about was how I'm going to kill Kia and watch her die slowly. She disrespected me for the last time and this time I'm going to smack her with a pistol and not my hand, Kia going to feel my wrath and that's on my life. About 30 minutes later we pulled up to Kandi house. I got my baby out the car seat and went int the house.

"Kandi, we need to talk," I said grabbing a bottle out of the baby bag so I could feed my baby.

"Okay, let me go take my shower and get into some comfortable clothes."

"Okay, but I actually need to talk to you and TK."

Kandi looked at TK, and he looked at her. "Okay, that's fine," Kandi responded.

They headed upstairs to get cleaned up. After I finished feeding my baby, I laid her blanket down on the couch, and she was passed out. Kandi and TK came downstairs and said they were ready to hear what I had to say, but I told them to give me about twenty minutes because I needed to take a shower also. Kandi gave me some pajamas to sleep in, and I went to the shower.

I turned on the shower and took my clothes off. As soon as I stepped in the shower, tears began to flow down my face. All I could do was cry. Just the thought of Gee laying in that hospital was driving me crazy. I don't know if he going to make it or not. I felt sick to my stomach, and before I knew it, I was hopping out the shower to throw up in the toilet. Everything was hitting me at once. I could go to jail for life if the police find out I killed Blaze. On top of that, I might be burying my husband. I pulled myself together and got back in the shower for another ten minutes then got out.

I went downstairs, and Kandi and TK were sitting on the couch waiting for me. Kandi handed me a glass of red wine when I approached her.

"What do you have to talk to us about?" Kandi interrogated.

I took a deep breath and prepared myself to tell them what happened.

"Well, I got a text from someone saying they had some information about Gee's infidelity."

"Oh my God, Shannon please don't tell me you shot Gee," Kandi yelled, holding her chest.

"No, I would never ever hurt Gee, Kandi! This is me you're talking to," I responded.

"Well, get to the point."

"I'm trying to if you let me, dang," I said.

I couldn't believe that Kandi would even have a thought like that in her mind, and when she said 'don't tell me you shot Gee,' TK gave me the nastiest look. If looks could kill, I would be dead right now. For Kandi to say that out of all people had me mad as hell. She knows I love Gee with all my heart and I worship the ground he walks on. I would never in my life pull a gun on him.

"To make a long story short, I met up with this person at 5555 Kirkwood Ave. When I got there, the back door was cracked open. I walked in, and the door slammed behind me. Blaze was standing there, and one thing led to another.

"What you mean one thing led to another?" TK interrupted me with his face frowned up.

I could tell from how TK was looking that he already knew what I was about to say.

"We ended up having sex."

"What? Shannon, have you lost your damn mind?" Kandi said with a serious attitude.

"No, Kandi, I didn't lose my damn mind. Can I finish the story?" I said as I took a sip of my wine.

"Go ahead," Kandi replied as she hit the Kush joint she was smoking and passed it to TK.

"Anyway, as she was eating me out, I felt a gun under the pillow. When she finished, I killed her. Not only did I kill her, but I also set her on fire along with the house."

"So, you telling me that you killed that bitch, Blaze?" TK said as he got up and walked into the kitchen.

I don't know what TK was going to do, but he had me nervous. I kept my eye on him.

"I'm glad you killed that crazy ass bitch because if you didn't do it, I would've eventually. When did that crazy bitch get out?" Kandi asked with a disgusted look on her face.

"I have no idea. That was my first time seeing her. I had no idea that she was out at all."

TK walked back into the room holding a bottle of champagne then popped it open.

"It's time to celebrate. I'm glad that stripper bitch is dead," TK said, holding the bottle in the air as it ran over.

I took the rest of my wine to the face and held my cup up for some champagne.

"Now tell me what's going on with this bitch Kia. Who is she?" TK demanded.

Me and Shannon broke it down to TK who she was and told him how everything started. From Gee sleeping with Kia to Kandi beating her ass twice and me slapping her ass. After we had finished telling TK the story and he learned that Kim and Kia were friends, he felt bad. I didn't even know TK was messing around on Kandi, especially with Kim's ass. This was news to me. I'm glad Kandi beat Kia's ass. Now she can tell her friend how we get down.

After everything had been run down to TK, he was ready to murder Kim and Kia. I told him I was down for whatever, and of course, Kandi was. The plan was for TK to kidnap Kia and bring her back to their house.

"I don't think it's a good idea for us to kidnap Kia and not Kim. I'm quite sure Kia told Kim what was going on, and we don't need no witnesses," I said, sipping my drink.

"Shannon, you got a valid point," TK replied.

We sat there in silence for at least five minutes trying to come up with a plan.

"I got it. How about you and Kandi go kidnap Kia while I game Kim to come over?" TK suggested.

"Don't sound like a bad idea," I replied.

"I'm down." Kandi agreed.

"Y'all sure y'all can handle this? We don't need no slip-ups," TK stated.

"Boy, you know I'm a G," Kandi said.

We all burst out laughing. "Yeah, bitch, we know you Scarface lil sister." We all chuckled.

I pick my baby up off the couch and took her upstairs to one of Kandi's extra bedrooms and laid her down on the bed. I don't want to take a chance of bringing Kia and Kim back to Kandi's house because my baby was here and I didn't want things to get out of hand, but we had no choice at all. We couldn't take them back to my house because I'm sure it's swamped with cops. I gave my baby a kiss on the forehead and said a prayer over her before left out.

When I walked out the room, Kandi was standing there with a black shirt and black pants in her hand. She handed them to me and told me to get dressed. Kandi went into her room, and I entered the bathroom and got dressed.

After I was done, I walked back downstairs, and TK was on the phone. He put his index finger over his lip, signaling me to be quiet. I sat down on the couch and listen to him spit game to Kim. I must say, he got game. I poured another glass of champagne as I waited for Kandi to come downstairs and TK to get off the phone. TK finally hung up about ten minutes later.

"Okay, everything is ready to go. I gamed her to come over here," TK stated.

"Well, I must say you got some game, TK," I replied.

"Well, you know I try to do what I can do when I do it," TK responded, acting like Chris Tucker on *Friday*.

We both fell out laughing.

"Kandi, come on," I yelled as I stood at the bottom of the steps.

"Girl, I'm coming. Don't be yelling at me," Kandi barked.

Kandi came stumbling down the stairs, and I could tell she was high and drunk.

"Kandi, baby, you sure you going to be able to handle this? You look wasted."

"Yes, TK, I'm sure. I'm not wasted, I'm just feeling good," Kandi said and grabbed her keys off the coffee table in the living room then walked to the door.

The way Kandi was stumbling to the door, I was convinced she was over the limit. Soon as she walked out the door, I snatched her keys and said, "I will drive."

We hopped into her car and pulled off.

TK

About twenty minutes after Kandi and Shannon left, Kim pulled up. I opened the door and flagged her to come in. Soon as she got to the door, she starts talking mass shit.

"I hope I don't have to beat nobody's ass today," Kim said as she walked through the door.

"Chill out, I told you she staying at her friend's house tonight. Plus, I got her key."

"Oh, that's even better because I would hate to be in jail tonight for beating her ass."

I wanted to slap her in her mouth for talking mass shit, but this would be her last day running off at the mouth anyway, so why not let her talk?

I chuckled. "You crazy."

"I'm not crazy. I'm just keeping it real. She thinks she's hard, but I'm harder," Kim fired back.

I ignored her and directed her to the living room, offering her a seat.

"Why you call me over here? Because you want some ass."

"Naw, because I want to see your beautiful face," I responded, biting my bottom lip.

"Umm hmm, niggas only want one thing, and that's some ass."

"Naw, them the lames you fuck with."

Kim gave me and lil fake giggle then said, "You think you got game." She laughed.

"You must think I got game." I laughed and took a seat beside Kim.

"Whatever," Kim said, rolling her eyes with a lil smile on her face.

She started rubbing my thigh, working her way to my dick. My dick instantly got hard. She gripped my dick through my pants and squeezed it.

"Umm, I miss this dick, TK."

"Show me you miss it," I replied, looking into her eyes.

She wasted no time unbuttoning my pants and pulling down my boxers. She spit on my dick head right before she placed her warm wet mouth on it. Kim jacked me gently as she moved her tongue all around my dick.

"Shit, suck that dick." I put my hand on the back of her head and moved it back and forth.

I can't lie, Kim had a nigga's toes curling, and I loved the shit. I mean, Kim has sucked my dick before, but this time she was putting it down. She must have taken some dick sucking lessons, classes or something. It's only person that made me bust off head, and that's Kandi. I pushed Kim's head back off my dick.

"Shit!" I yelled.

"What's wrong? You can't handle this tongue?" Kim stood up and pulled her dress up and her blue thong down, and sat right on my dick.

I know what I was doing was wrong, but it felt so damn good. Plus, after today, I won't be fucking her no more anyway.

Kim started bouncing up and down on my dick slowly as I held her hips. The juices were splashing all over me. I removed my hands off her hips and placed them on her ass. I repeatedly smacked her ass, and she started going crazy on my dick. I couldn't hold my nut any longer, and I nutted all up in Kim.

"Fuck, that pussy was good," I said, smacking Kim on the ass.

"No, that dick was good. TK, I love you."

I knew right then and there I was going to have to kill this bitch. She said the four-letter word, love. Ignoring what Kim said, I got up and put my boxers and pants back on.

"You want a glass of champagne?" I asked.

"Sure," Kim said with an attitude.

"What's wrong with you?"

"TK, I said I love you, and you didn't even bother to say it back."

"That's because we haven't even known each other long enough to love each other." I walked into the kitchen and left Kim on the couch.

I poured two glasses of champagne, then I got the sleeping pill I had stashed in the kitchen drawer and crushed it up in her drink. I went back into the living room and handed Kim her drink.

"Cheers," I said.

"Cheers to what?" Kim barked.

"Cheers to us, baby. Drink up."

We both took our drinks back. About ten minutes later, Kim began to look woozy, and before I knew it, she was passed out. I picked her up, threw her over my shoulder, and took her to the basement. I duct taped her mouth and tied her feet and hands together.

Shannon

When we pulled up to Kia's house, there was a pizza delivery man leaving. When we saw that we were clear to approach her house, we got out the car and headed to her door. Me and Kandi both had pistols on us. Kandi had the duct tape and rope also. I told Kandi to put her gun up because she had too much shit in her hand and she was already drunk. I knocked on the door, hoping that Kia didn't ask who is it or I was going to have to disguise my voice.

The door swung open, and I cracked Kia in the head with the pistol. She fell to the ground and was out for the count. I shut the door, and we tied her up and taped her mouth. I told Kandi I would be back.

I pulled the car into the driveway, and we threw her body in the trunk. After we were done, we locked the bottom lock on the door and left. On the way back to Kandi's house, she was throwing up the whole way. It damn near took us an hour to make it back to Kandi's house. Every five minutes, I was pulling over for Kandi to throw up. We finally made it back to Kandi's house. I had to literally hold Kandi up to get her in the house. When we got in the house, I laid Kandi down on the couch. She was only half awake.

"TK, where you at?" I said, trying not to be too loud.

"I'm down in the basement," TK replied as he came upstairs.

"Did y'all get her?" TK asked.

"Yes, she's in the trunk. I had to bring Kandi in because she was throwing up on the way back."

"I knew her ass was too drunk to go, and she smoked that Kush joint to the face." TK shook his head.

"Well, come on. Let's go get this body out the trunk and get it over with," I commanded and walked to the door. TK trailed behind me.

When I opened the trunk, Kia was still knocked out. I felt her neck to see if she had a pulse, and she did. TK grabbed Kia out the trunk and took her straight down to the basement. When we made it to the basement, Kim was on the floor crying and trying to wiggle her way out the ropes. TK threw Kia's body right next to Kim.

"Which one you want to kill first, Shannon?"

Soon as he said that Kia's eyes popped open. When she realized where she was, she began to cry.

TK handed me a pistol with a silencer on it. *Pow,* I shot Kia in the leg.

"I want to make her suffer first," I said, looking down at Kia as she suffered from the bullet wound I put in her leg.

I bent down and removed the tape from Kia's mouth.

"You got anything you want to say?" I asked, standing over Kia and aiming the gun at her head.

"Fuck you, bitch," Kia said, barely talking.

"No, fuck you and your life. Did you really think you were going to get away with shooting Gee?" I questioned as tears filled my eyes.

"I should've killed your ass when Blaze told me to."

"That's why Blaze is blazing in hell right now. I killed her just like I'm about to kill you."

I laughed in my evil voice and shot her in her other leg.

The look on Kia's face was of devastation and pain. Since Kia wanted to talk shit, I'm about to show her what happens when she sleeps with someone's husband.

I walked over to Kim and pointed my gun at her head. With no hesitation, I let off two shots, instantly killing her. All Kia could do was scream and cry. She knew her life was about to be over. I walked back over to Kia and stood over her.

"Please don't kill me. I'm sorry, Shannon," she pleaded.

"Sorry ain't going to get my husband out the hospital bed," I said and shot Kia in the head.

"Let's clean this shit up, ASAP," TK stated as he put his joint out.

We wrapped both of the bodies up and carried them to the car. We put them in the trunk and drove to a wooded area nearby. TK got out the car to make sure it was safe to dump the bodies. Next, we grabbed the bodies out the trunk, dumped them in the woods, and left. I had no remorse for what we just did. The whole night I slept like a baby.

The next morning, I woke up took a shower, fed my baby, and slipped back into the clothes I had on the night before. I asked TK and Kandi to keep an eye on my baby while I went to check on Gee. Kandi was laying on TK's lap with a hangover. I just looked at her and laughed. I left and made my way to the hospital to check on Gee.

"Good morning, what room is Gee Hightower in?" I asked the nurse at the front desk.

"He's in room 447 on the fourth floor," the nurse replied.

"Okay, thank you."

I rushed over to the elevator and pressed the up arrow. When the doors opened, I got on and pressed four. I prayed until the elevator dinged, letting me know I was at my destination. I strolled down the hall until I found room 447 and opened the door. When I walked in, Gee was lying there with his eyes wide open.

"Baby!" I said excitedly as I ran over and kissed him all over his face.

Gee cracked a smile, and a tear dropped from his left eye.

"I love you, I'm sorry, baby, for everything I've done," Gee said in a raspy dry voice.

"Shhh, baby, you don't have to apologize. Let's just put everything behind us."

"I'm with that."

Gee was released from the hospital three weeks later, and we now live happy and drama free.

The End